ORAIÁPHON

Marian L Thorpe

Arboretum Press

This one's for you, Brian.

THE WORLD OF *ORAIÁPHON*

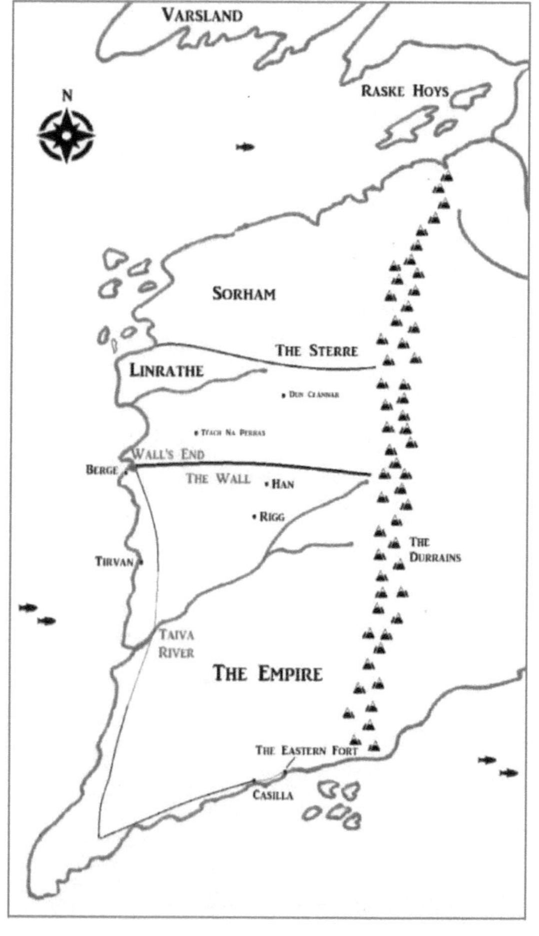

AUTHOR'S NOTE

The events of *Oraiáphon* begin almost immediately after the Battle of the Taiva, the penultimate scene of *Empire's Exile*. I hope it will please readers who asked for more of this part of the story, and provide context to the central conflicts of *Empire's Reckoning*, the next book in the series.

'Oraiáphon' is pronounced *or **eye** ah phon*, the emphasis on the second syllable. In this world, we know the same mythological character as Orpheus.

Orpheus with his lute made trees,
And the mountain tops that freeze,
Bow themselves when he did sing:
To his music plants and flowers
Ever sprung; as sun and showers
There had made a lasting spring.
Every thing that heard him play,
Even the billows of the sea,
Hung their heads, and then lay by.

Shakespeare; Henry VIII

CHAPTER 1

"THE SCOUTS REPORT NO MARAI within Linrathe," the soldier said. "There are still skirmishes along the Sterre, but those are diminishing, and appear to be mostly defiance and bluster, *Teannas'óg*."

"Thank you," Ruar said, dismissing him. *Teannas'óg*, they called him, young leader, after his calm and thoughtful leadership during the fighting against the Marai. Hard to believe, I mused, that he was not yet fourteen. Donnalch had taught him well.

His regent, his great-uncle Liam, grunted. "You need to ride north, Ruar. Be seen by your people," he said.

Ruar turned to me. "Will you accompany me, Lord Sorley?"

I should. This was my country's leader asking me. He hadn't been formally recognized as *Teannasach*, but there was little doubt that would happen. The Marai were in retreat, so we must have won, but the rumours from the Empire were confused and contradictory; nothing official had reached us yet, here in the camp hidden among the hills and valleys of Linrathe. Almost everyone I loved was somewhere in the Empire, and I did not know if they were safe.

"You do not need me, Ruar," I prevaricated. "I cannot even play for you, just now." I had taken a sword wound to my left arm; nothing serious, and already healing, but it did prevent me from holding a *ladhar* comfortably.

"But you are my friend, Sorley," he protested. His great-uncle scowled. The *Raséair* did not approve of me, although he had grudgingly praised my efforts in bringing Ruar north, and in the fighting. Talk of my choice of men as my bedmates had reached Liam's ears, I assumed. I wondered, sometimes, if it was one of the reasons my father had supported the Marai, knowing we would be on opposite sides, and ensuring our family's lands went to my younger brother Roghan, and not to his *channàdarra* oldest.

Distant shouts reached my ears. I looked up, frowning, just as the tent flaps parted and a soldier entered. "My pardon, *Teannas'óg*," he said, "but there is a rider come from the south, looking for the Lord Sorley. He has dark skin, and speaks no Linrathan, nor much of the Empire's tongue. He is very agitated."

Druisius? Fear rose. "Excuse me, Ruar," I said,

following the soldier toward the perimeter of the camp. I saw Druisius with the guard, pacing impatiently, and broke into a run. "Druise!" I shouted. "What has happened?"

"Cillian," he called. "He is badly wounded. Lena needs you. Why are you still here, Sorley? Did not the messenger sent from the Taiva reach you?"

Cillian. He should have been safe. If he was wounded— "No messenger," I said. "What of the Emperor?" I'd reached Druise now.

"The Emperor Callan is dead," Druise said, frowning at the bandage on my arm. "Traitors, within his own army. Cillian would be dead too, except the Emperor blocked some arrows with his own body. But not all. Come, Sorley. There is no time to waste. You are hurt?"

"Just a cut," I answered. "But what happened?" A twisting, inside: I'd liked Callan.

"I will tell you as we ride," he said. "Gnaius says he will die from infection. Lena will not sleep, barely eats, will not leave him. She is making herself ill."

"Dear gods," I said. Cillian, dying? No, my mind said. No. "She is pregnant, Druise."

He swore. "She will lose the baby," he said bluntly. "We must ride, Sorley."

"Find us fresh horses," I told the guard. "Now. And food and water, enough to get us to the Wall. Ten minutes. Druise, come with me. I must tell Ruar what has happened."

Fifteen minutes later we were riding south, at speed. Ruar had given me leave, immediately. As I turned to go, he stopped me, a hand on my arm. "Lord Sorley," he said, his young face serious. "I swear to you I will do all I can to regain Sorham and your lands. Believe me in this. I will right the wrong my uncle did."

I didn't really care, at this moment, but a response was needed. "I do believe you, Ruar," I said. "I wish you success."

"There may be a place for you in that fight, some day," he replied.

"If I can be of use, I will be," I said, rote words. My mind was not in this wind-shaken tent, but long hours south and west, at Wall's End. I would have said almost anything to speed my leaving.

Druisius shouted the story at me as we rode: Kebhan's treachery, the Lestian archers within the Empire's army swayed by his promises, the betrayal of the drum codes to the Marai. "Lena killed Fritjof," he told me. "Her arrow, in his neck. Junia had killed his son, minutes before. It was all that saved us, those two deaths."

"Is Cillian really dying?" I asked. I could not bring myself to believe it.

"He is not in this world, and his skin burns to the touch," Druise answered. "Gnaius says only the gods can save him."

Cold fear battled with dull resignation for the rest of the long ride. We switched horses at the first guard post we reached on the Wall, and twice or three times again. I half-slept in the saddle, once we were on the road that paralleled the Wall, rousing only when my horse slowed.

We rode into Wall's End not long after dawn. I slid off my horse, my injured arm aching. I could barely stand. I realized that Druisius must be in agony: he was a foot-soldier, not cavalry, but he had been riding at speed for over three days.

I turned to Druise. "Go," he said.

"Where?"

"The sick rooms." I turned to the guard who had opened the gate.

"Where?" I asked again. He pointed, explaining. I tried to run, forcing my legs to move.

More questions, inside the building, and then I was in the room. Lena slumped in a chair, her hand holding Cillian's. His chest rose and fell shallowly. She did not look up. "Lena," I said.

She raised her head. Huge dark shadows swallowed her eyes, and her face was thin, far too thin. Her hair spiked and clumped on her head. "Sorley," she whispered.

I knelt beside her, trying to hold her. She shook her head. "Talk to him," she rasped.

"Help me hold on to him, please, Sorley. Please." I put my hand over hers, and Cillian's. His fingers were white and his flesh cold, but the flush of fever stained his cheeks.

"Cillian," I said, my voice catching. "Cillian, it's Sorley. I'm here. Can you hear me?" Tears pricked at my eyes. Oh, gods, Cillian, I thought. Don't die. Please don't die. I felt Lena's hand clench mine, and heard a deep, racking sob.

"Sorley," she moaned, turning suddenly to hide her face against my shoulder, sobs tearing through her. I pulled her close with one arm, the other still holding Cillian's hand.

"I will fetch Gnaius," I heard Druisius say. I hadn't heard him come in. He and the doctor returned in a few minutes. Lena still wept.

"How have you let her get to this state?" I growled at Gnaius in Casilan. "She is pregnant. Did you not know?

"I did," he replied gravely. "But she has refused whatever I have offered, and even an order from her *Princip* was ignored." He bent to her. "Tell her," he said, "that she must think of the child. His child. She must sleep, or risk losing it."

I translated. She shook her head. "Lena," I murmured. "I will stay with him. I promise. Druise will find an instrument, somewhere, and I will play music for him, and talk to him. But you must sleep."

She shook her head again, but less vehemently. "You promise?"

"I do. Let Gnaius give you a sleeping draught." There was a cot against the wall. "You do not even have to leave the room."

"See if she will let someone take her to the baths," Gnaius whispered. "I will give her a mild dose of poppy now, and a bit more after, to make her sleep."

"No," Lena said, when I suggested it.

"Tell her I will take her," Druisius said. Highly irregular, I thought, but what did it matter? I relayed his offer. She looked up.

"Just for a few minutes," I said. "You do need the baths, Lena." She stank of sweat and fear.

"Oh," she said. "All right. No one but Druisius, though."

"Who is here that can permit this?" I asked Druise. "The baths will have to be closed to all others." I kept glancing at Cillian, watching for each breath.

"I will find someone," he said. Gnaius, at a side table, prepared the first dose of poppy.

"She is to drink this." He held it out. Lena took it, her hand trembling. She swallowed it, making a face. Druisius came back, with, of all people, Casyn.

"General!" I said in surprise.

"I was on my way here to see how Cillian did, and Lena, this morning," he said gravely. "What is it Druisius is asking?" I explained. He turned to Gnaius, making writing motions. The physician gestured him to the table. Casyn wrote a note, quickly. "Take her," he said to Druisius, holding out the note. "He is in good hands, Lena," he said to her softly, as Druise led her to the door.

Casyn's eyes went to Cillian. "The hands of the

gods, the physician says," he murmured. I turned to Gnaius.

"How is he, truly?" I asked.

"If the gods love him, he might live, but I doubt it," he said. "I can do little." My heart clenched.

I told Casyn what Gnaius had said. He nodded, reaching out to touch Cillian gently. "I will pray," he said simply. "He is a soldier, too. I am glad you are here, Lord Sorley. I must work, now."

Work. I remembered something Druise told me as we rode. "*Princip*," I said. "I apologize, for how I greeted you earlier." He was Callan's heir, and now the *Princip* of the Western Empire.

"No matter," he replied.

I had barely slept for over a day, but I kept my promise to Lena. I sat beside Cillian, holding his hand when I wasn't playing the *cithar* Druise had found me. I played, and I talked and sang in Linrathan: if anything would reach him, I thought, it would be his own tongue. When I had to leave, for the minutes it took to relieve myself, Druise took over. Even when Gnaius or the fort's medics came to wash and turn him, and to drip liquids or poppy juice mixed with wine into his mouth, I stayed. I saw the terrible wounds on his back and thigh, and the red streaks of infection. I made myself endure it all, although the moans of pain Cillian made tested my self-control to its limits.

"His eyes may open," Gnaius told me. "He may

speak. It will not make sense. He may see things that are not here, but not that which is. But if he begins to thrash about, or tries to rise, do not let him, and send someone for me, immediately."

More than a day passed before Lena reappeared. She had slept the entire time, exhaustion assisted by the sleeping draught. Clean and rested, she looked marginally better than the day before. I stood up, swaying with my own fatigue, when she came in. She knelt, unspeaking, to kiss Cillian on his chapped lips, murmuring to him.

"Thank you," she said, looking up at me. "You should sleep now."

"Baths first," Druise said from the cot where he had been dozing. "Then some sleep, and then the two of you take turns, yes?"

"Yes." Her hand went to her belly. "Yes, all right. The cadet is outside the door, if I need someone to go for Gnaius?"

Druisius checked. The boy was there. I bent to kiss Cillian's forehead, feeling the heat of his skin. "Stay with us, *mo gràhadh*," I whispered. As I turned to leave, Lena put her hand on my arm.

"It is all right, Sorley," she said. "I need you to love him, and to tell him that you do. Maybe with two of us loving him so much, we can keep him in this world. Maybe the gods will see, and take pity on us."

I put a hand on her shoulder, and bent to kiss her cheek, fighting dizziness as I straightened. "Maybe they will." I couldn't find anything else to offer hope. I couldn't see any hope.

"Come," Druise said. I followed him to the baths, stumbling more than once. In the antechamber, he undressed me and sponged me down before leading me into the steaming water. Had he done this for Lena, yesterday? I supposed he had.

A wine flask and cups had appeared on the table in my room. From where? Wine must be in short supply; did I rate it because I was the lord Sorley, or because I was thought to need it? Did I care? I poured two cups, not watering mine at all. I drank it, quickly, and poured more.

"Sorley," Druise said, concern in his voice. We had been lovers in Casil, for a few weeks. I had told him the first night that I loved Cillian, but in our casual, temporary pairing, what had it mattered?

"Don't tell me not to," I said bluntly. "I need it, Druise. He is going to die, and there is nothing I can do, or Lena, or even Gnaius, it seems."

"Maybe not."

I drained my wine cup and threw the cup against the wall. It shattered, the sound clear and sharp in the still air of the room. It didn't help. I took a deep, shuddering breath. "I can't even be there all the time. Gods, Druise, I still love him—and I'm sorry, I know I shouldn't say that to you—and I can't take it. I must leave—Lena stays, sleeps there, eats there—and I've only been here a day. Why am I so weak?"

"You are not weak," he said, putting an arm around me. "Lena believes she can keep him alive by her will, her love. That is why she will not leave. You do not think that, in your heart."

I leaned against his solid strength. "No," I admitted. "I don't. Perhaps the music eases him, and it cannot hurt to talk to him, but will it save him? I don't think so."

"Sleep now," he urged.

"You must be exhausted too. Don't you need to sleep?" I yawned, hugely.

"I have slept more than you might think, this last day." A ghost of his grin came and went. "Maybe I stay?"

Fatigue and wine fogged my thoughts. "Stay?"

"The bed is wide. Better than the barracks."

"But..." I had just reminded him I loved Cillian. Why was he offering to stay? "Can you?"

"No one cares where I sleep."

"If you want." I couldn't work this out right now. I sat on the bed, pulling off first my shirt, and then the soft indoor shoes. That was enough. I lay back. Sleep claimed me before I had finished pulling up the blanket.

When I woke some hours later, the blanket was fully over me. In the blackness of the room I could hear soft snores. Where—? Memory asserted itself, and with it fear. I stifled a whimper with my hand. A moment later I felt fingers on my back.

"Sorley," Druise whispered. His hand moved, his lips nibbling at my neck. I felt the pulse of response. But I shouldn't, not now, not with—Druise bit my shoulder, not quite gently, and I whimpered in a different way and rolled over.

I couldn't call what we did making love. I gave into a need to extinguish fear and death in the demands of hands and tongue and sex, and there was nothing gentle or loving about it. I didn't recognize myself, not in what I did or what I allowed—anything not to think—and when it was done and I lay limp and breathless, hollowed out, Druise put one hand on my belly and kissed me on my lips.

"Did that help?" he asked. He ran his fingers down my cheek, a gesture that spoke of tenderness. Only a few minutes earlier that same big hand had held both my wrists in a trap-like grip. "Better to use anger," he said. "Even as we just did."

"I'm not angry." He chuckled, drily.

"You are," he said. "Sleep again, *amané*."

"I can't," I said, but I was slipping towards a welcome darkness. His hand still rubbed my back. "Druise," I murmured, "Why…?" I didn't hear an answer.

CHAPTER 2

I WOKE MANY HOURS LATER, alone, to find an older man quietly placing a tray of soup and bread on the table. "Sergeant Birel, isn't it?" I asked. Casyn's soldier-servant.

"Yes, my lord." I looked around. My clothes had been draped over a chair, the breeches on top. I hoped Druise had done that, and not Birel.

"Do you know where Druisius is?" I asked.

"In the infirmary, sir, with the Casilani physician. He acts as translator. The *Princip* asks if, once you have eaten, you would speak with him briefly. He said to tell you that he will not keep you from the Major's side longer than necessary."

The Major. Cillian's rank. He was still alive. "I will return shortly," Birel said. I ate the food—I was hungry, I discovered—and drank a little wine, well-watered. Then I dressed in the clean clothes I found on a stool, combed my hair, and waited, trying to think about what Casyn might want, and not what I had done in the night. Birel returned promptly. He led me through passages to a tall door, knocked once, and opened it. Casyn and Turlo were bent over maps. "Lord Sorley, sir," Birel said, ushering me in.

"Sorley," Turlo said. "Good to see you, *mo charaidh*, even though—" He didn't finish the thought, just shook his head helplessly. No one expects Cillian to live, I thought. And regardless, the work of the *Princip* and his advisors must go on.

"My lord Sorley," Casyn said gravely. "I will be brief. There is work that would have fallen to Cillian that I wish you to take on. I cannot command you, as you are Linrathan; I ask as your *Teannasach's* ally. There are letters to write, to Casil, before the ships sail home; that is the first thing. I also would appreciate your thoughts on some questions I have about the Marai, but that can wait. The letters are more urgent, as the Casilani ships prepare to return home before the winter gales prevent them."

"I will do my best for you, *Princip*," I said. "But I have not the fluency in Casilan that Cillian has, nor the diplomatic turn of phrase."

"Aye, well," Turlo said. "You can begin with a letter, in Casyn's name, telling the Empress why it is you that is writing. She will forgive any awkwardness of phrase or fluency under the circumstances, I believe."

"Eudekia will be distressed," I answered. I thought she would be; for all her playing of diplomatic games, she had genuinely liked Cillian, had enjoyed his learning and wit and the agility of his mind.

"Aye," Turlo said. "Perhaps."

"When would you like me to write these letters, sir?" I asked Casyn.

"Could you relieve Lena at Cillian's bedside for a few hours, then return to us once she has eaten and rested? Two or three hours should see them done, and then you can go back to the infirmary. I understand she has agreed to take better care of herself, if you are with Cillian," Casyn added. He eyed me, assessing. "My brother told me of the child," he said quietly. "It brought him great joy. It will be, in part, why he tried to protect Cillian from the arrows."

In the sickroom, nothing had changed. Druise wasn't there, and I was relieved by that: I didn't know what I'd say to him.

Lena agreed to a few hours rest, but she went no further than the cot against the wall. I sang and played more than I talked. Somewhere in those hours my fingers strayed to the melody of *An dithës braithréan.* "Not that one," Lena said, from the cot.

"No?" I answered. "Has not war separated us?" There were tears on my cheeks again. I put the *cithar* down, burying my face in my hands.

"Sorley," Lena said softly, coming to me. She leaned against my back, her arms around me.

"It is so unfair," I said. "He was truly happy, for the first time in his life."

"I was wrong in Casil," she said, "thinking what he did there was his descent to the underworld. This is, Sorley, and the god will want to keep him. We have to keep calling to him, to remind him he is loved and must return."

"Do you really believe that, Lena?"

She shook her head. "I don't know. Gnaius does, and perhaps he is right. I am willing to believe anything, if it makes him live."

Dagney, I thought, would say that the story is about the strength of love, and its power to change people. Cillian moaned softly, his head moving from side to side. "Shhh," Lena murmured, taking his hand. "He told me once that his best memory was of his grandmother singing to him, when he was very small," she said to me. "Sing the songs she would have, Sorley. I cannot."

I sang Linrathan lullabies, and they did seem to soothe him. When Gnaius came in with the next dose of poppy, he raised an eyebrow in surprise. "He is very calm," he said to me. "He should be more distressed, from pain. What have you done?" When I told him, he nodded. "Very good," he said. He paused. "That tells me he hears, sometimes. Music and speech are not the same, but be careful of what you say near him. Nothing that will trouble him."

Lena put a hand on my shoulder. "Go to Casyn now."

"You will send for me, if he becomes restless, and music might help?"

"I will," she said. A cadet stood outside the infirmary door, half-drowsing, but there to run for the physician if needed. Or for me.

"A moment." I kissed Cillian's forehead, ran a finger along his jaw, thick with stubble. I glanced at Lena. She nodded, almost imperceptibly. I crouched, my lips close to his ear. *"Thà mi gràh agàthe*, Cillian," I murmured. "We both do," I added, still in Linrathan. "Come back to us."

I wrote the letters Casyn requested, first the one of explanation, then the ones of thanks and appreciation, ending with an estimate of the threat the Marai still posed and the measures being put in place to counter it. There would be Empire's troops on the Sterre, with the Linrathan ones, I learned, and ships on the coast, too. When had Ruar—or Liam—agreed to this?

"They haven't, yet," Turlo said, when I asked. "I ride north soon to make the proposal. I trust Ruar will see the sense in it. I would ask you to come, Sorley, were there not other demands on your time."

"I would have sent Cillian," Casyn said, quietly.

"Neither of us should have been sent," I told them. "Ruar trusts Cillian, but Liam does not. None of that house did, I believe, because his father was thought to be from the Empire. Now it is known that he is Callan's son, Liam would trust him even less, I believe."

"And you?"

I tried to find words to explain. Turlo rescued me. "The southern vice, I believe is the term, in Linrathe and Sorham."

"By the god," Casyn said, "as if whom you bed matters. But it ties my hands, Lord Sorley, if your own countrymen will not respect you. I had hoped you could be an envoy for us."

"I am Linrathan," I reminded him. "I could not be your envoy. But perhaps you could request of Ruar that I be Linrathe's envoy to the Empire?"

He frowned. "Would they do that? If they have no liking for you?"

"Ruar calls me friend," I told Casyn. "It is Liam who wants nothing to do with me, and more importantly, wants me to have no influence on Ruar. But he also, grudgingly, respects what leadership I provided against the Marai, and that I kept Ruar safe. I think he might see the position as a way both to reward my efforts and keep me away from Ruar and out of Linrathe for much of the time."

"Excellent," Turlo said. "I will make that argument, with your leave, Casyn?"

"Perhaps," the *Princip* said. "I have other questions yet." He paused, studying me. "One thing, Lord Sorley. There will be much to talk about, between Linrathe and ourselves, if we are to present a united front against the Marai, assuming

Casil allows that. You may have to be away from here, some of the time. Can you do that?"

"Not yet," I said. I had to be honest from the start, if I were to work with this man for the good of both our lands. "I would leave Cillian only under protest, just now. My presence, or rather my ability to sing the songs of his childhood to him, cradle tunes, calms him, it appears. Relieves his pain, perhaps. Nor would I leave Lena, by choice. She needs a friend, and I am one."

"Aye," Turlo said. "That you are, and more, to both of them. But the hard truth, Sorley, is that it cannot be long before we know. Cillian must begin to recover soon or die. By the time I return, I should think."

I returned to the sickroom to let Lena go to the baths and rest. I watched Cillian's chest rise and fall; he'd been dosed with poppy, Lena had told me, and should sleep for some hours. He'd be too deeply unconscious for music.

The wound on my arm hurt, but it was only a tight itchiness, a sign that it was healing. I rubbed it gently.

The door opened. I looked up. Druise. Well, I had to face him sometime. He came over, unspeaking, to lay fingers on Cillian's skin. "Not much fever," he said.

"Gnaius gave him poppy and willowbark, an hour ago," I told him. He nodded, and touched my shoulder, gently.

"Wine?"

"A little," I said. He poured and watered the cups, handed me mine. "So," he said, sitting. "My story. I am from the *subura*, the second son of a minor merchant. I have three sisters, one brother; those who lived, anyhow. I did not want to be a trader, so I joined the army." He drank some of his wine. "I was a pretty boy. I caught the eye of an officer. This happens, you understand? But I did not mind. He was kind, and the food better and the room warmer."

Why was he telling me this now? I didn't know what to say, but he didn't seem to expect a response. "He was killed fighting the Boranoi. I fought and lived. Then another officer, and then another. The last gave me my post at the palace as a present, when he retired to his villa. To keep me safe, he said."

"So he cared about you."

"Yes. All did, I think."

"Did you love any of them?"

"Love? No. I liked the first man best. He could play the *cithar*. He taught me about music and bed." He stood to fetch more wine. "We have things to learn together, yes?"

Heat rose in my face. "What can I teach you?"

He chuckled. "About music, much. The other, when you have learned more about yourself, perhaps much there, too. But your question last night? I do not know. Why does any man like what he likes?"

"Oh, gods," I said. "I wasn't—I didn't—" I took a breath. "That wasn't what I meant, Druise."

"No?" He held out the wine flask. I shook my head. "What, then?"

"Why are you here? Shouldn't you be with your regiment?"

"My captain at the Taiva did not come north. I came with Lena, without permission. No one questioned it."

In the chaos after the Taiva, that did not surprise me. A missing soldier would be presumed to be dead, I supposed. "It is a good thing you did," I said. "But Casyn and Turlo know you are here, surely?"

"Of course. The General Turlo sent me to find you."

"Then I think you are his to command," I said. "Perhaps this should be straightened out? Cillian needs you. Lena needs you."

The next day I listened as Casyn elaborated on his thoughts about the Marai. In his letter to the Empress, he had said he thought that they would be disorganized for some time; with both Fritjof and Leik dead, it would take some time for a new leader to emerge. He hoped, he told me, to take advantage of that, but that he needed me to help him.

"How?" I asked. I could pass as Marai, just, my pale hair and blue eyes indicative of northern ancestors, but I might be known to some who had traded with my father. I said as much.

"No," Casyn said, "not that sort of help. I simply need you to be my translator." He stopped, grimacing. "This will sound harsh, Lord Sorley, and I do not mean it that way, but Cillian's loss will have repercussions beyond personal grief. We need his skills, with language and diplomacy, and if by some miracle he lives, it will still be long months before he might be capable of the work. Turlo speaks your tongue, but not that of the Marai or Casil. It is why I need you, do you see?"

"I do," I said. "I will do what I can, *Princip*. My Marái'sta is good; my Casilan adequate, I suppose."

"That will be enough," he said. "Can you go down to the harbour later today? The Casilani captains have questions that we cannot understand."

I agreed. Birel came in, quietly, but without knocking. "Will the Lord Sorley be joining you for the midday meal?" he asked.

"Yes," Casyn said, "if he likes. My lord?"

"Thank you," I said. "*Princip,* could we dispense with my title? I am unused to being addressed this way."

He grinned. "Certainly, Sorley, except when protocol requires, but only if you too call me by my name. Agreed?"

"Agreed," I said. "I will be pleased to eat with you, Casyn, if you will excuse me afterwards. I should let Lena rest, and play for Cillian while his noon dose of poppy takes effect."

"Anything you can do to ease my nephew's pain, or the strain on Lena, must be a priority."

"Tell me, Sorley. What is the man who is regent for Ruar like? I know little of him," Turlo asked, as we ate the simple meal. "Did he support Lorcann?" I thought back to the months I has spent travelling through Linrathe, gathering information, carrying messages, letting those whom I believed I could trust know that the *Ti'acha* would provide shelter and food to anyone opposing Lorcann and the Marai. Liam's name had come up once or twice, but never with anything definite to be said about him, or his allegiances.

"Liam did not publicly support Lorcann," I said. "The *Teannasach* is chosen from within the family, by all the men of blood or marriage over eighteen. When Donnalch was murdered, there was no time for that; Lorcann simply announced he was now *Teannasach*. He may have been the second choice when Donnalch was proclaimed; I do not know. But Liam is conservative in his thinking. He may truly not have approved, or he may not have thought it appropriate to voice that support without the formal acclamation."

"Think, Sorley," Casyn urged. "Did Cillian ever say anything that might tell if we can rely upon him to be our ally?"

Had we ever spoken about Liam? A memory played around the edge of my mind...the ship, on the way to Casil. "Turlo," I said, "you were there. Did he not just say that Liam would be the likely regent, for either boy?"

"Aye," Turlo said. "Not much help."

"If he agrees to me being envoy, I will be required to go to them, to receive their instructions. I could gather more information, on the way. Do you trust me with this, *Princip*?" I murmured.

"I think I must," Casyn said. "But I will ask some hard questions now, Sorley. You will forgive me for quizzing Turlo yesterday about your character: I must know the man I am entrusting with our secrets." I nodded. Of course he must, and Turlo would have been honest. "Cillian called you his dear friend, but he is more than that to you." Not a question. "Were I not *Princip*, but only regent for Cillian, where would your loyalties lie? To Ruar, or to him?"

I had come to Cillian from Ruar's side without thought or hesitation. Did not my actions tell the story? "My heart tells me Cillian," I said. "But I made Ruar a promise." *If I can be of use, I will be*. I had made one to Lena, too, that I would always be by Cillian's side. I couldn't think about that right now.

"You will have to swear an oath to him if he appoints you as envoy, will you not?" Casyn asked.

"No. Linrathe has a long tradition of neutral

envoys, serving the country and not the man leading it. It is the exception to the oaths we swear. That is why Cillian was not sworn to Donnalch: I did not understand that, until he explained it to me. *Toscairen* are supposed to be detached, observers and recorders only; one of their roles is to gather opinion from all the *torps*, and that will not be given freely if the *toscaire* is known to be loyal to a particular man."

Even as I spoke I knew I was not telling the entire truth. Cillian had not just listened; he had spread ideas in subtle ways, hints and suggestions, I guessed. Whose ideas? I'd never wondered, before.

"And is your...loyalty to Cillian known in Linrathe?" Casyn probed.

"Not by anyone who would use it to cast doubt on me as a *toscaire*," I answered. Perras knew, and I guessed Dagney, but they would never reveal my secrets. There was no one else, unless my father had realized, all those years earlier, why I had been so adamant about going to the *Ti'ach na Perras*. But my reasons—that it was the best school for me to learn music and the *danta*, with the elder *scáeli* of Linrathe as its Lady and teacher—had been credible, and I did not think he had a moment's comprehension of my other motive.

"Then," Casyn said, reaching a decision, "I will trust you to make the judgement regarding Liam. All this, of course, depends on Turlo's skills of persuasion in convincing the man to appoint you *toscaire* to the Empire."

"You are riding to the Sterre?" I asked Turlo.

"Aye. That is where you said they were headed."

"Then the *Ti'ach na Asgaill* will be the closest *Ti'ach*. Asgaill—if he lives—can bear witness to what I did for Linrathe during the Marai occupation, and you, Turlo, can speak to the work we did together for both our lands. They would be further reasons for Ruar to argue for this appointment. Ruar and Liam may even be using that *Ti'ach* as their base."

"Well-reasoned," Turlo said. "I will leave tomorrow. There is much haste to be made, with the year moving toward winter. I would like to be home before the snows."

If he was leaving that quickly— "General, may I ask a question? Druisius—he has no assignment, is that right?"

"Has he not?" He thought about it. "His regiment went back to the Eastern Fort. Did he have his captain's permission to come north?" I hesitated, and he gave me a hard look, before breaking into a grin. "Don't worry, *mo charaidh*. I don't care at this moment. What has he been doing?"

I explained. "He is a very good nurse, it appears. Is there a way to assign him to the medics?"

Turlo shook his head. "I could. But even before the Taiva, was he not translating a little?"

"Some, yes. And he does for Gnaius now."

"Then we need him for more than nursing

duties." He tapped a finger on the tabletop. "Would he accept being a soldier-servant? If so, I will assign him to Cillian; a major is entitled to one. He can do what is needed for him, and still be free part of the day for other duties. Send him to me."

I thanked him. He cuffed my shoulder, gently. "An officer's soldier-servant sleeps nearby, to be close if needed. Your room is not so far that he cannot be easily sent for."

My room? I must have looked puzzled. "He is your *consor*, isn't he, lad?" Turlo asked.

"*Consor*?"

"Partner. It is our practice to know when a relationship between men is not just casual, so we consider it in deployment. Isn't that why Cillian asked for him to be released from his palace duties, so he could come west with you?"

"I see," I said. "I suppose it was, yes." But why had Druise agreed? I had some sense now of how poor a lover I must have been in Casil, inexperienced and tentative, and worried about what was being reported back to the palace. Did he really want to be my partner? In music, perhaps.

We talked further of the road north, and what Turlo could expect to find at the Sterre. Then I excused myself and went to sit by Cillian so Lena could rest. Gnaius had dosed Cillian with poppy earlier, Druise told me. "I will turn him now, when he feels little pain," he said. "You will help me?"

I did what Druisius directed me to, settling Cillian on his uninjured side. He moaned, unseeing. I brushed his hair back from his face. "It needs cutting," I said, "to keep it out of his eyes."

"I will cut it, when I wash him later," Druise said, propping pillows on either side of Cillian. How had he learned to be such a good nurse? Cillian moaned again, but it sounded more like a sigh, and less like a cry of pain. I took his hand.

"When Lena comes back, will you accompany me to the docks?" I asked Druise. "The *Princip* has asked me to find out what the Casilani captains want. And Turlo wants to see you, as soon as possible."

Outside, the stones of the fort gleamed in pale sunshine. It had rained earlier. Druise walked beside me as we made our way to the steps that led down to the docks. A commotion at the southern gate caught my attention. A soldier, and from the look of her lathered horse one who had ridden at speed. She ran for the headquarters. I did too, not knowing why: an instinct. We met outside the *Princip*'s workroom, just as the guard opened the door.

"*Princip*," the soldier said, saluting. "I am to tell you a ship has been sighted, sailing north, flying the Casilani flag, sir. There are two smaller ships accompanying it."

"How far away?"

"We were on the headland south of Berge," the scout said, "and the ships were distant. Two hours, perhaps? The winds are favourable."

"Thank you, soldier," Casyn said, dismissing her. "Lord Sorley, who might this be?"

"I have no idea," I said. "But I will find out."

CHAPTER 3

HALF AN HOUR LATER I was back at Casyn's workroom, and not alone. "*Princip*," I said, indicating the man with me, "this is Rufin, captain of the Casilani fleet. He tells me the approaching ship is almost certainly carrying a Casilani official, the Procurator. His name is Decanius."

"The Procurator?" Casyn replied. "What is his job? And why was I not informed officially?"

"His job is one of great responsibility and great power, *Princip*," Rufin told him. "He is to ensure Casil's laws are put in place, at least those governing the army, and taxation, and certain resources."

I tried not to look shocked as I translated for Casyn. How had we not known this? But Rufin answered my unspoken question. "Cillian was aware of this man; we spoke of it as we sailed west."

Cillian, I thought, would have seen this as his responsibility, to be discussed with the Emperor and his advisors. But that meant Casyn should have known, and I could tell from his expression he had not.

"What will he expect when he arrives?" Straight to the point, no time wasted in futile questions.

"A formal welcome; the best rooms you can give him, and the best food. He is the Empress's representative, *Princip*."

"And in terms of my time?"

"Much of it, I am afraid. I am only a ship's captain, *Princip*, and this is beyond my experience."

"And mine," Casyn murmured. "Ask him what Cillian thought, please, Sorley."

"It is not what they spoke of," I relayed, "except that Cillian said he would want access to records here, to prepare for the discussions."

"Why is Rufin telling us this?" Casyn asked. "What is his motive?"

I asked. Rufin smiled. "Tell the *Princip*," he said, "I like it here in these western lands. There is space, and so much sea, and if this coast is to be patrolled and protected against the threat from the north, a fleet will be needed. It will need a commanding officer, and I would like to be that man. A recommendation from the *Princip* might help, and," he paused, "the man appointed as Procurator likes to promote his friends. He does not count me among them."

Casyn grimaced. "Tell us about him."

Decanius, Rufin told us, had been second to the

procurator of another province east of Casil. Competent enough, from all he had heard. "He is well-connected," Rufin commented. "His mother's brother is Quintus, advisor to the Empress."

Quintus, who had advised Eudekia not to support our plea for help; who had tried to bribe Cillian with citizenship and lands and was possibly the mind behind the attempt to kidnap Lena. Whose opposition had led Cillian to offer himself to Eudekia as her consort, if that was what was needed to seal the alliance. Even I could make these sums add up.

I explained, quickly, to Casyn. "Eudekia must have agreed to give him this position to allay Quintus's opposition," I told him. "He will be reporting back to his uncle, I would think."

"You are almost certainly right on both counts," Casyn said. "Tell the captain he has our thanks. Ask the guard to find someone to escort him back to the docks. I need you to stay with me, Lord Sorley."

The *Princip*, I discovered, could swear creatively and at length—and some of his invective was directed at his dead brother. "Callan's mind was on defeating the Marai," he muttered. "He would have planned to deal with this man and the terms of the treaty once the war was over. And yet again I am left to clean up the aftermath of his thoughtlessness." He grimaced. "But to the task at hand. This man wants to catch us unawares, I would say. Birel!"

"A formal meal," he told his aide, when he appeared a minute later, "the best we can produce, for this evening. For perhaps ten or twelve. The best wine. See to it." He turned to me. "And now you must teach me to greet the Procurator properly in Casilan."

I went over Casyn's words of formal greeting with him one last time, correcting his pronunciation. Then I left him, going first to the infirmary. I told Lena and Druisius the news. Druise eyed me critically. "You need a shave."

I felt my chin. "I suppose I do," I said. "I better do that now."

"I will," he said unexpectedly. He shaved Cillian, I knew. "This man will notice."

I hoped Birel thought the same. Casyn's chin had shown grey stubble, this morning. I touched Cillian's hand. Cold, as always. But his nails were neatly trimmed, and the skin as smooth as the unguents Lena applied could make it. The small attentions of love.

In my room I sat with a towel draped around my shoulders as Druise shaved me, competently and closely, the scrape of the blade against my throat making me shiver. When my jaw and upper lip were smooth, I took fresh clothes from the chest, shaking them to remove the creases before changing. Druise watched, half amused, half appreciative, I thought. He clicked his tongue. Bending, he picked up my boots, scuffed and worn. I had no others. "I can fix these," he said.

"Druise," I protested. "You are not my servant."

"Friends help each other, yes?" He put the boots down and left the room, returning in a few minutes with something in his hands. As I combed my hair and shrugged on the cloak, managing not to stab myself with the pin of the brooch, I watched him working at the leather of my boots with grease and a flattish piece of bone. I could see the scratches and scuffs disappearing as he worked. Did all soldiers know this trick? By the time he was done, the boots shone.

I pulled them on and stood up. "Lord Sorley," Druise said, grinning.

"Will I impress the Procurator?"

He snorted. "Decanius? Certainly not."

Casyn too was freshly shaven. Dressed in the grey-and-white of his office, his silver pendent catching the sunlight, he appeared to me completely calm as we waited on the jetty. The rowers brought the ship in; ropes were thrown, commands shouted. We stayed well back, out of the way, watching. Its captain disembarked, with a man of middle height, balding, stocky. Rufin, who had been overseeing the ship's docking, joined them.

"Come," Casyn said to me. We approached the captain and his companion.

"*Princip*," Rufin said, "may I present the Procurator Decanius."

"Procurator," Casyn replied, his Casilani pronunciation acceptable, "be welcome. I am Casyn, *Princip* of the Western Empire, by the grace of the Empress Eudekia."

"Lord Sorley of Linrathe," I said, as we had agreed. "I act as translator for the *Princip*, Procurator. May I too welcome you to Wall's End?"

Decanius inclined his head. "*Princip*. Lord Sorley. May I extend my sympathies, *Princip*, at the death of your brother, the last Emperor. And his son?" Something in his voice, the tone of it, told me these questions were formalities. He didn't care.

"Is gravely ill, Procurator. The prognosis is poor. I thank you for your sympathy and your concern," Casyn replied, through me.

"Shall we proceed to the fort, Procurator?" I asked. "You might wish the baths, after your voyage?"

"Baths!" he said, "Baths and wine would be most welcome." As we climbed the steps to the fort, I noticed Decanius stopped more than once to catch his breath, although he claimed to be looking at the view. "Well-situated," he noted. "What is the village I can see?"

"Berge," I told him. "A women's fishing village."

"Women?" he said. "So close? How interesting." He puffed his way to the top. The guards at the gate, their weapons gleaming, saluted. He ignored them.

"I will have the baths to myself?" he asked, but it wasn't a question. I assured him he would.

"Ask the *Princip* to join me," he said, "and you, of course, Lord Sorley, as we cannot communicate without you."

"Of course," Casyn said. "Will you show the Procurator his room, and then we will meet at the baths?

Decanius said nothing about his rooms, situated on the floor above the workrooms and lesser bedrooms. He was happy to see the wine jug. I poured him a cup; he did not offer me one. He went to the window, nodding appreciatively at the view over the training fields and the glimpse of the jetties, and the sea beyond. Shedding his cloak, he tossed it on the bed. If he expected me to hang it up, he was disappointed. I already didn't like him, although I could not have said exactly why. He had been polite enough, but he looked *through* people, I thought, unless he believed them to be of some use. In Sorham and Linrathe, every man and woman had value, their own worth to the estate, and Casyn treated all his soldiers in the same way. Perhaps, I mused, it is because there are so few of us, on both sides of the Wall. Could you value everyone, in a city as crowded as Casil?

But this was not Casil. Birel—I supposed it was Birel—had ensured the Procurator's arrival was known to all the troops, including the cadets, and he was saluted respectfully by all ranks. I acknowledged everyone with a nod or a word, purposefully. If I appeared a barbarian in the Procurator's eyes, I thought, better that than Casilani indifference.

At the baths Decanius behaved no differently, accepting the assistance of the attendant without a word. In the hot pool, he looked around him. The pool and walls were unadorned, unlike Casil's baths. "It serves its purpose," he said. "A modicum of comfort in this northern land."

"Tell him," Casyn said, after my translation, "Wall's End, like the Eastern Fort, is a military complex, and that I am sorry if he is not as comfortable as he would have liked. We will attempt to rectify that, as best we can."

"There is one thing," Decanius said in response. "I am in need of a woman. Or a boy, I suppose."

I am just the translator, I reminded myself. Casyn's face remained impassive, although I could hear the control in his voice when he spoke.

"Procurator," I said. "You must understand that both men and women in the Western Empire choose their own bed partners, and that cadets—male or female—are not permitted to consort with adults. If a woman of Wall's End decides to be your lover, that is her choice, and cannot be coerced."

Decanius looked decidedly put out. In Sorham, I thought, a man of his rank would have been offered a serving woman as a matter of course. It was part of their duties, although they could refuse, and children born of a night with a visiting *Harr* were accepted into the *torp* without question. But this was not Sorham, either.

"I see," he said. "How uncivilized. What about the women from the fishing village?"

"Casyn," I said, "he must know what the Marai did to the women here. Should I remind him?"

"Please."

"My lord Decanius," I said, "the women of Berge, and all the villages, have the same freedoms. But you are unlikely to meet with a welcome there; you will recall the violence they have endured at the hand of the enemy Casil helped us defeat."

"But there are Casilani troops who have chosen to remain?"

"A very few, yes," I told him.

"And as they are Casilani, I may—interact—with them as I wish," he said. The muscles of Casyn's neck tightened.

"Of course," he said.

"We should also discuss the composition of the army," Decanius went on. "There are irregularities in your command structure that must be remedied. I have asked one or two of the officers who came to remain, and I have sent for others."

"Perhaps," Casyn said, "that discussion should wait, Procurator, until the General Turlo, who was in Casil, and my other advisors can be present? We are not accustomed to deliberating matters of policy in the baths. We prefer to speak of lighter things. Do you play *xache*, Decanius?"

"I have been known to," the Procurator said, "with an opponent of sufficient skill. Is there a library here?"

"A small one." On my own initiative, I added, "If it is books you wish, Procurator, I can request some to be sent from the school I attended. Some of Casil's philosophers, and Heræcria's too, although in translation to Casilani."

"Do so," he said. "I must say I am grieved to know the Emperor's son is so unwell. From what my uncle told me of him, I was hoping to discuss philosophy with him. Although he does not speak Heræcrian, of course."

"We too grieve his health," I said, not waiting for Casyn's reply. "He has been my friend for nearly a decade, and his *quincala* is pregnant. I pray the child will know its father." I had been abrupt. "We are grateful for the expertise of the physician Gnaius in attending to Cillian," I added.

"Gnaius." Decanius brightened. "Is he still here? I expected he would have returned home. I look forward to his company."

Somehow both Casyn and I remained calm and polite for the rest of the time in the baths. After I had shown Decanius back to his rooms and assured him someone would fetch him shortly for the meal, I went back to Casyn's workroom.

"If," he said, "we did not need all our wits, I would be drinking unwatered wine just now, and offering you a cup too. Have you ever met anyone so self-interested, Sorley?"

"It fits with what Rufin told us."

"You had better have Druisius warn the Casilani troops of the Procurator's interest." The Princip spoke briskly. "I am surprised, to be honest, he does not have his own servant with him, or a slave to cater to his wants. Or is that not done in Casil?"

"I am not sure," I said. "Should I ask Druise?"

"It would be useful to know," Casyn said. "Such a relationship between an officer and his soldier-servant is not uncommon here, although it is of course by mutual agreement."

I opened my mouth to ask, closed it again. It was none of my business. "So if a Casilani soldier agrees?"

"If so, and the Casilani officer raises no objection, then I suppose the soldier can be assigned to the Procurator as an assistant. Even one of the women, although that will certainly raise eyebrows." Whereas, I thought, a man would not. Still almost incomprehensible, to me.

Casyn had been pouring wine as he spoke, although he made liberal use of the water jug. Handing me mine, he took a sip. "I wonder what Birel has instructed the kitchen to prepare?" But my thoughts were not on food.

"Casyn? Does Decanius have any authority over

Druisius?"

He put his wine cup down. "Druisius is under Turlo's command, at this moment. But in truth, Sorley, he could be considered guilty of desertion from the field. It is unlikely to be discovered; the officer who commanded his regiment has returned to Casil. We can simply say a verbal secondment was made, that there was no time to write an order in the aftermath of the battle, if Decanius ever asks. But I doubt he will care about a simple soldier."

Nor did I, upon consideration. Druise was one of the men the Procurator would not even see.

CHAPTER 4

"I WISH TURLO HAD NOT ridden north." Casyn exhaled, loudly. "I know nothing of how Callan might have responded, or what Cillian thought," he said, pacing the room. "I have only you, Sorley."

"I am no diplomat," I protested. "Only a musician, trained for little else except managing an estate."

"You spent almost five years at the school where Cillian learned his skills, did you not? Are you being modest?"

"No." How to make him understand? "The same school, but not the same learning. I came to the *Ti'ach* to learn more about music and story. Some history, yes, and the languages were mandatory for us all, but I was not taught the skills to be a *toscaire*—an envoy—as Cillian was. I meant to be a *scáeli*, a bard, I think you would say."

"And your lover? The Casilani? Can he help us understand the intricacies of Casilan politics?"

"I am afraid not, *Princip*. He was only a palace

guard. But," I added, the idea coming to me, "the physician, Gnaius, might have more insight. He has been highly placed, both in the Casilani army and in the palace, I believe."

"Then we must speak to him. Bring him to me later this afternoon, if you will."

I should go to Cillian. But my head ached, and I needed time alone, to consider all that had happened, and all that was being asked of me. I found Gnaius, who told me he would be pleased to speak to Casyn after he had seen his patients. An hour, he said, maybe a little more. I had time for the baths.

Several other men were in the hot pool, but after polite greetings they left me to my thoughts. I closed my eyes, leaning back against the side of the pool. Slowly my mind stopped flitting from idea to idea, and settled on one concern. Druisius.

I didn't know what I wanted—or rather I did, at least in one way—but was it fair to him? How could I sort out my feelings for him just now? Cillian was going to die. I was trying to help Casyn understand a treaty I knew too little about, and comfort Lena, and now I had to translate for this unpleasant Procurator.

Turlo had taken it for granted Druise was my partner; he knew we'd been lovers in Casil. I'd thought then I was learning to love Cillian differently, as a friend, an illusion shattered the moment Druise had told me he was dying.

But it had been Cillian who had asked if it would please me if Druise came east with us. He had thought our shared love of music would overcome the differences of upbringing and language...and experiences, I knew now. He'd liked Druise, and he had wanted me to be happy. Wasn't that all the answer I needed?

I collected Gnaius from the infirmary and took him to Casyn. The wine, I noted, was of better quality than earlier.

"Before we begin," Casyn said, sitting across from us, "is there any change in Cillian?"

"None," I said, listening to Gnaius. "The fever does not abate."

"What are the treatments?"

"Poppy to make him sleep, anash against the infection, other drugs for the fever," I relayed. Casyn nodded. He asked about a few other injured men—a shock to me, the reminder that Cillian was not the only man Gnaius was treating—before turning the conversation to politics.

Gnaius stroked his beard with one finger. "The *Princip* wishes to know what a Procurator does?" he clarified. "He is responsible for taxes and rents and pay to the army." Casyn wrote that down. "He will bring surveyors, and they will be sent out immediately to do a census and map the roads and villages. And to find the deposits of metal ore, and where salt could be made, and grapes grown."

"This falls under his jurisdiction?" Casyn asked.

"Yes. As does pay to the army, and therefore its organization, *Princip*." Gnaius sipped his wine. "This was not made here," he commented.

"No doubt it is from Casil," I said. "You are being honoured by it."

"Decanius is the man who will implement almost all the details of the treaty with the Eastern Empire, then," Casyn said.

"Exactly so," Gnaius agreed. "May I say more? I have lived in many of Casil's provinces over the years. A physician travels with the army, if he wishes to become a skilled surgeon. And from my days at the palace I know somewhat of Decanius's family, and what they strive for. I believe Decanius will be looking for opportunities to enrich himself and his friends." The physician raised a groomed eyebrow. "There is nothing unusual in this, you understand. It is what most men want, including myself."

Casyn put his pen down. "Is Gnaius asking for money?" he asked bluntly.

"The *Princip* wishes to know if you require further compensation for your work."

Gnaius looked genuinely surprised. "No," he said. "The Empress pays me well. My enrichment here comes from the challenges of healing, and what— when the men I tend can safely be left—I will learn from the healers of this land, and what I can teach them. But," he added, smiling, "if the *Princip* is offering, more of this wine would be welcomed."

I laughed, as did Casyn when I told him Gnaius's answers. "Tell him I will have Birel send him a supply, in appreciation of his skill."

Gnaius bowed to Casyn, and waving aside my offer to escort him, left me alone with the *Princip*. "What do you remember of the details of the treaty?" he asked immediately.

"Some," I said. "I read Cillian's translation on the ship, and I was there when he and Turlo explained it to you and the Emperor. But I paid more attention to the details affecting Linrathe, *Princip*."

"Understandable." He leaned back. His face, lined by fatigue, was troubled. "I have been concerning myself with all that a general must after losses such as we took in the last year. Our army is in considerable disarray; we have too few officers, and not enough men—people, now some women wish to remain as soldiers—for the regiments. We need horses, and feed and fodder for the coming winter, and food for ourselves, and the women's villages that supplied these are mostly gone."

"But is that not what Gnaius said Decanius will also be concerned with? The reorganization of the army, and a survey of the land? Surely your concerns are not so different, *Princip*?"

He pursed his lips. "Perhaps not. When we conquered Leste we sent officers to do the same there and made their king a nominal governor. Is that what I will be, Sorley, a voice for this Procurator, and nothing more?"

"I don't know," I said helplessly. "Cillian did. Does. What he and the Empress discussed privately—only he knows that. Maybe he told his father. He did not tell me."

"Did he tell Lena?"

"I don't know," I repeated.

"She is with Cillian? Then let us go and ask her. I need to move, and I have not seen him for a few days."

In the infirmary Lena sat holding Cillian's hand. He lay motionless, pale, breathing shallowly, his hair—Druise had cut it, I noted—lank and lifeless. Lena looked little better.

Casyn put a hand on her shoulder. "May I speak to you?"

"Do I need to leave him?"

"No. We will not disturb him, I think," he said gently. I pulled a stool close to the opposite side of the bed, reaching for Cillian's other hand.

"I'm here, Lena. Talk to Casyn."

I stroked Cillian's hand, forcing myself to listen to what Casyn and Lena were saying. "No," she replied, in answer to his question, "he did not tell me. I am sorry, Casyn, but I know nothing of the treaty beyond what is written."

"It was a hope," he said simply, but I heard the

disappointment. "I wish," he said, "my brothers were not dead. We need Colm's knowledge, not just Callan's ability to make connections, and his subtle thinking." For a moment he stared past us, his eyes hollow, unfocused. "But we cannot change the circumstances," he murmured. He took a deep breath, squaring his shoulders. He looked down at his nephew. "May the god bring you back to us," he said. "You are needed. Stay here if you wish, Sorley, but come to me in the morning."

"He never wanted to be anything more than a blacksmith," Lena said, after Casyn had left us.

"What?"

"Casyn. He told me that once himself, and Turlo did too. He felt he had to be at Callan's side, to advise and guide him, and Callan wanted to lead. Was meant to, Turlo said. He said the same about Cillian." Her voice held no emotion at all.

"The men from the ship do not like this Procurator," Druise told me as I played quiet music for Cillian, in the hour before midnight.

"I'm not surprised," I said.

"I did not either, in Casil. Be careful. He has power, *amané*."

"He wanted a woman. It was almost the first thing he asked for. A woman, or a boy." I remembered what Casyn had wanted to know. "Would he not typically have a servant, or a slave, to meet his needs?"

"Yes. Perhaps he thought a barbarian would be interesting," Druise said. I caught the slightest hint of a grin.

I gave him the expected response. "And am I?"

"Very," he said, his teeth flashing in the dim room. I remembered, with a sharp twinge of desire, the blade near my throat as he'd shaved me, earlier. "I saw the General."

"And?"

"Soldier-servant," he said, "That is amusing."

"Why?"

"You were not to know. It is what I was called, in Casil. To my officers. So I could share their tents."

"You didn't tell the General that?"

"Of course not. Am I an *idióta*?" He adjusted Cillian's pillow. "Even if he recovers, it will not be me he wants in his bed. Maybe you and I, we need to talk. Before I move my things to your room, as the General thinks I will."

Be careful what you speak of near Cillian, Gnaius had said. I motioned Druise away. "What do want to say?" I asked, when we stood against the far wall.

"I like you," he said. "We are good together, yes? The music, and in bed. I will be your *consor*, if you want."

I glanced over at Cillian. "Even—?"

"My first officer, the one I liked the most? His marriage was not political. He loved his wife. So this is not new to me, Sorley. But I want an agreement."

"What sort of an agreement?"

"About what I see and hear. Do not kiss him, not on the lips, or tell him you love him, if I am there." He smiled, wryly. "For him, you do this already. That is why we moved away from the bed, yes? In case he could understand what we talk about?"

I spread my hands helplessly. He was right, of course. "Are you sure?"

"If you wish. If you can do what I ask." All I saw on his face was patience, like a man waiting for an answer in a business transaction he knew was favourable.

We made good music together, and I wanted him in my bed; he made me feel things no man before had. Cillian was dying. Druise would help me forget.

"I can," I said.

On the bed, Cillian moaned, his head moving on the pillow. His eyes opened, but there was no recognition behind them. Druise went to the sideboard, unlocking a drawer. He brought the poppy syrup over to the bed, and expertly propping Cillian up, spooned the dose into his mouth.

"Play," he told me. I had stopped, watching in concern. I chose a cradle tune, one of the first melodies I had learned. When Cillian was quiet again, Druise arranged the pillows. "Go and sleep," he said.

"I promised Lena."

"I will be here. She trusts me with him now. You have important work to do in the morning." He spoke matter-of-factly. "This is my job, Sorley. When Lena returns, I will give him more poppy. Then I will come to bed. And awaken you, *amané.*"

"All right. Do you want the *ladhar*?"

"Why not?" He grinned. "A good time to practice, while the poppy takes Cillian to oblivion." I touched his shoulder in farewell, smiling, but inside I was unsettled. The word Druise had used did mean oblivion in Casilan, but it also meant a river of the underworld, a river the dead drank from to forget their earthly lives.

"The Procurator," Casyn told me, the next morning, "has no wish to meet with me for at least a week. He must confer with the Casilani officers first, it appears."

"About what?" I asked.

"Army matters, no doubt. But it does not displease me, as it gives me time to read the treaty, line by line, and discuss the meaning and the interpretations that can be made of each point, and prepare arguments. It is what Colm would have suggested. But he also taught me that one point of view is not enough. Will you spend a few hours with me each day doing this? Not more than two or three: I have other matters that must be dealt with."

"I will," I said. "But am I the right person? I know little of your laws and customs, *Princip.*"

"I am sending for Jereme: he is—was—at Casilla, with the youngest cadets. I do not even know if he is still alive: he was already old, before the war. But he was Colm's teacher, although the student quickly surpassed the master. Even so, it will be some weeks before he arrives. I must review the treaty before then. I had a mind to include my daughter Talyn as well; much of the treaty will affect the women's villages."

"It is her son who will be *Princip* after you?"

"Faolyn, yes. He is nine this year."

"Perhaps his father, then, as well?"

Casyn laughed. "I don't know who his father is; Talyn does, of course, but she has never told me. And he is more likely—if he is alive—to be an unranked soldier than an officer."

I flushed. "Forgive me, *Princip*. This is new to me."

"Different customs. Ways of thinking." He gave me a considered look. "Other aspects of life here must also be new to you, and welcome, I should think?"

I understood him immediately. "Does no one think it wrong? What I am?"

"Wrong?" He was genuinely puzzled, I saw. "Sorley, in this land men and women lived separately for all but two weeks a year, with no Festival for the men until they were eighteen. If you can find me a man here who tells you he has not taken pleasure with another man, whether for a night or two or in a longer relationship, he is either a liar or an ascetic. For some men it is casual, for some it is their nature, as I understand it is yours. But wrong? How could it be?"

Was he telling me he had—? I tried to assimilate this. "My father," I said, "would have disinherited me. Would still, if he knew."

"I am sorry for that," he said after a moment. "There is a parallel here, you know, with our sons who will not or cannot fight. Colm suffered that fate."

Turlo had told me—not about Colm, but about the practice—on our travels. "It might be a good thing," I said, "that Cillian grew up in Linrathe."

"Callan said the same," Casyn said. "He did not see Cillian as a soldier. And yet Colm died protecting the Emperor, and Cillian may die from wounds suffered on a battlefield. Courage comes in many forms, Sorley, and only men blinded by prejudice and thoughtlessness think otherwise." He smiled, sadly. "Can we begin analysing the treaty?"

I was glad to escape to the infirmary. Gnaius was there, dripping drugs into Cillian's mouth. He nodded at me but didn't speak. I picked up the *ladhar* and began to play.

Gnaius straightened. "Go," he told Lena, who obeyed him, to my surprise. To me, he said, "Keep playing." I looked away as the physician undid the bandages. I heard him click his tongue.

"I will prepare poultices," he said to Druise. "Wash him. I will not be long."

I could not watch Druise's hands touching the man I loved so intimately. It confused me. I walked to the small window, concentrating on the instrument. I heard Druise moving, the splash of a cloth in water, his tuneful humming of the melody I played. He murmured to Cillian occasionally, his tone calm, reassuring.

Gnaius, true to his word, was back quickly. "Good," he said to Druise. "We will turn him onto his stomach now. Remove these poultices when they cool. Come with me: I will teach you to make them. Apply them four times a day and tell me when the wounds begin to drain."

Druise was gone for perhaps half an hour. He checked the poultices first when he came back, before coming to pull a stool up beside mine.

"He is very ill," he said.

"The wounds fester?" I knew they did.

"Deep inside, Gnaius says. Maybe the poultices will draw it out. Maybe not."

"Does Lena know?"

"Yes. Gnaius tells her the truth. But she will not leave his side, except while the wounds are treated, and that only because Gnaius insists. Or if you are here, or sometimes me, now."

If I was going to do everything Casyn wanted of me, I wouldn't be able to be at Cillian's side as often. "It is because of her vow to him," I said. "He was alone, for so long, Druise. She told me he had never known, before her, what it was to wake with someone beside him." I swallowed. "She swore he would never wake alone again. So she, or someone else who loves him, has to be here."

"There is no one else? From his land?"

"Dagney," I said, and an idea came to me. "Maybe she would come. She and Perras, and Perras could assist Casyn: he knows as much as Cillian about Casil and its laws. I will write to them." Even as I spoke I realized I didn't know if they were alive, they or anyone associated with the *Ti'ach*. My mind recoiled at the thought of more loss.

"Do not tell Lena," Druise said, "until you know this woman will come. She cannot take more disappointment."

CHAPTER 5

IF YOU CAN FIND ME A MAN here who tells you he has not taken pleasure with another man, I will show you a liar. I couldn't stop thinking about Casyn's casual words, the implication—no, the admission—that he had had male lovers. That nearly every man in this fort, this army, this land had. The shameful secret I had hidden for so long in Sorham was just a normal part of life here. My mind felt dislocated, untethered.

Every pair of soldiers I saw laughing together, every casual touch I witnessed made me wonder. I was embarrassing myself, acting like a boy newly aware. Which is what I was, I supposed. I'd told Druise what Casyn had said, swearing him not to repeat it. "So?" he'd said. "Most armies, I think. But more so here, because the boys are together from so young." He'd kissed me, then. "Better than hiding, yes?" he'd said, and we'd stopped talking.

We hadn't repeated the desperate, furious

coupling of that first night at the fort, but he was teaching me things I hadn't known about myself. I'd had little experience, before Druise: a few men, mostly musicians. Brief encounters, furtive and frightened. Now for the first time in my life I felt no judgement, real or imagined, and no fear, although what I was learning about what gave Druise—and me—pleasure did shock me, a little.

Still, I hated myself, sometimes. Watching Cillian slowly die was shattering my heart, and my nights with Druise were an escape. Guilt wracked me, too: what solace was there for Lena? Nor was Cillian the only anguish in my life. Dagney's reply to my letter had added to my grief. Perras had been days from death when she wrote, a lung infection slowly choking him.

'But he understood what I told him: that you and Cillian had returned safely from Casil,' she had written. 'Knowing that, and about Cillian and Lena and the expected child brought him peace. He had worried for you terribly. I did not tell him of Cillian's wounds. He does not need to know.

'When he is gone, and we have mourned him and buried him, perhaps I will come. I might be some comfort to Lena. There have been no students at the *Ti'ach* for some time, and until there is a new *Comiádh*, I may choose not to teach. It will be difficult without Perras.'

I had to stop reading at that point, blinded by tears. Only later did I pick up the letter again, to read the rest.

'You asked for help with understanding Casil's history, and with the language. You must know Cillian was Perras's best pupil in many years in those disciplines, but there were others. But who is alive, and who Ruar and his advisors might allow to be sent is unknown to me. I will enquire.'

The letter had contained a separate note, addressed to Lena, and a postscript.

'Sorley, on consideration, I will come south when I can, if the *Princip* will allow it. I cannot teach Casilani, but I can teach Linrathan, and Marai'ista, if those are of use. It will be better for all of us if we who loved and honoured Perras and Cillian are together, I believe, and the approaching birth will bring us hope.'

I took the note to Lena. She read it, smiling briefly. "She asks me to tell Cillian she loves him," she said. "I already have, long ago, but I will again."

I beckoned her away from Cillian's bed. At the far side of the room, in a whisper, I told her about Perras. She closed her eyes in pain. "Both his real father, and his foster father," she murmured. "I liked Perras, so much."

"Dagney says she will come, to be with us," I said. "As soon as she feels able. She says the child will give her hope."

"She is a reason to live," Lena said. "When he dies, Sorley, she will be the only one I have."

I had never heard Lena admit that Cillian was going to die. I put my arms around her. "I will be here," I said. My own acknowledgment of the truth. She sobbed, once, then took a deep breath and pulled away.

"I shouldn't leave him." She went to the bedside to pick up his limp hand. "Cillian," she began, "there is a letter from Dagney."

We had spent the last week reviewing the treaty, Casyn and Talyn and I, making notes and a list of questions for Turlo when he returned from the north. Then we had compared the structure of the Empire's army with that of Casil's, with help from Druise, at least for the land army. The differences seemed minor to me: the size of cohorts and regiments, the rank at which one was considered a senior officer, rather than a junior. Titles that would need redefining, as they meant different things in each army.

"One other," Druisius said. He was remarkably comfortable in the presence of the *Princip*, I noticed; respectful, but not overawed or obsequious. Then again, I reflected, he had been a palace guard. What was the western Empire's *Princip* when compared to Casil's Empress?

"And that is?" Casyn enquired.

"In Casil, women are archers only. Their own

cohorts, foot and horse. They do not mix with the men. In any way," he added.

"I hadn't realized that," I said. I remembered Lena telling me of Junia's surprise when she had learned Lena was partnered with a man. This would explain it. I would have to tell her, someday.

"We need the women throughout the troops," Casyn said. "We do not have the numbers, without them."

Druise shrugged. "The Procurator will argue, I think."

"What do you know of him?"

"I was part of an escort for him, once or twice. He does not thank his guards or consider them in any way. Other officials had us sent water, or allowed us shade, if we had to wait at midday. Not Decanius."

"That," Casyn said, "tells me quite a lot. Thank you, Druisius." Druise saluted and left.

"It will be interesting," Casyn said to the room, "to hear if the Casilani officers tell me the same as Druisius has."

"A bright man," Talyn commented. "I suppose—and forgive me for this, Sorley; I know he is your lover—that we can trust him?"

I bristled, instinctively, but it was a question that had to be asked. "Yes," I said. "But not for that reason. His appointment as Cillian's soldier-servant is not the first time he has held such a post." In some form, at least. "He has always been completely loyal to his officer, and he will be now."

"Birel," Casyn said, "tells me the same, that he is protective of Cillian, and Lena, and not, I am assured, just because of the circumstances. Birel has been with me for a long time, and I trust his judgement in this."

"I will not argue with your sergeant," Talyn said. "I was only wondering where Druisius can best be used, when—when Cillian no longer needs him."

"As a liaison with the Casilani men," Casyn said. "We have Sorley to translate for the officers, but if we have no one to hear the men's thoughts and complaints, we will have a dangerous situation."

"He will need a minor promotion, for that."

"When it is appropriate, yes," Casyn said. "But promoting him too quickly will breed discontent among our own troops. You may tell him that, unofficially, Sorley, if you think it worries him."

"Druise," I said, "worries about very little. But you have reminded me: I have had a letter from my *Ti'ach*." I explained who Dagney was, and what she had written, accepting their words of sympathy regarding Perras. "May she come?"

"Of course," Casyn said. "If for nothing but to comfort Lena, she would be welcome. But lessons in both Linrathan and Marai'ista are a good idea; it is a pity she cannot teach Casilan. But I am less happy with the thought of other Linrathan men teaching our officers: to echo Talyn, can we trust them?"

"Why could you not?" I asked.

"There was significant support for Fritjof within Linrathe, was there not? Has your *Teannasach* demanded an oath from all who survived the war? And even if he has, men have given such oaths falsely."

"Before I joined Turlo," I said, "I was part of those who worked against Fritjof. All the *Ti'acha* were involved, so if the man—or woman—suggested is someone I or Dagney know also did that work, will that ease your concern?"

He rubbed his chin, considering. "It will," he decided. "As a teacher only, though, although a second translator would be useful. But I will need to judge them for myself. You must continue to translate in our meetings with the Procurator."

"Translate, not negotiate," I countered. He nodded.

"Translate only. I do not expect you to argue our cause, Lord Sorley. Now, shall we look at the implications of separating the women into separate cohorts? This was our original practice, before the war with the Marai, after all. We must have all the arguments in place to counter the Procurator's."

CHAPTER 6

IMPORTANT WORK IT MIGHT BE, but translating was also incredibly tedious. For days we discussed in minute detail the composition of the Empire's army, land and sea; then in the same detail how Casilani troops were organized, armed, and led. Turlo grew so impatient and testy Casyn sent him away, back to the Sterre. Talyn, newly promoted to a captain's rank to give her sufficient seniority to be Casyn's advisor, joined the talks, along with the *Princip*'s adjutant, Michan. Michan was quick with languages, picking up Casilan rapidly, at least the military terms. A good thing, too, as I did not always know the right words.

Decanius had found a soldier to be his scribe—and perhaps more—and at the end of each day I checked his notes, then ours, looking for discrepancies. When I found one, as I almost always did, it engendered more discussion. Decanius had claimed the baths for himself and his invited guests for an hour in the late afternoons, so Birel served us wine after the Casilani had left us. The water jug remained full, most days.

We compared sizes of cohorts: twelve in Casil, ten here. It became twelve, plus the cohort-leader, no longer a junior officer but a rank below that of sergeant. A *capora* for every two cohorts; a sergeant for every four. A new rank, subaltern, below lieutenant, and together these were the only junior officers. Captains became senior officers.

"This is necessary, you see," Decanius told us, "so that the pay is correct."

"Pay is one thing," Casyn said, "but I do not see how we have the men and women to do this, even if we collapse some of the cohorts, as we must."

"A temporary situation," Decanius said. "In the spring Casilani troops will fill the vacancies, especially among the officers."

Would they? Quintus had been opposed to sending any troops to our aid, given the aggression on the Eastern Empire's borders. I must remember to tell Casyn this, I thought.

"While we are discussing the troops, there is another irregularity to be addressed," Decanius said. "Women have only one role in the army: that of archers, horse or foot. Not mixed among the troops as you have them."

"That may be true in the Eastern Empire," Casyn said carefully, "but here our women have different skills: blacksmithing, carpentry, masonry. All needed, to maintain the fortifications, and the roads, and to shoe our horses and repair our harness and weapons. We cannot waste that expertise, Procurator, and nor can we afford to remove men with the same skills from their work, to ask them to ride patrol or guard the gates when women can do that equally well."

"It is not protocol."

"It is here," Casyn said. I translated his words; his tone of voice would be understood. "The women of our Western Empire have earned their places in this army. Without their defence of the villages three years ago, we would have fallen to Leste. Without their willingness to join our troops, Linrathe, when it was our enemy, would have overrun us. Their numbers too were essential in keeping the Marai from total victory as we awaited Casil's aid. Three times we have needed them, Procurator, and we have a saying here: the third decides. Our women will do the work our officers assign. Not what you think is appropriate."

Decanius's bald head flushed. His toe tapped. "Very well," he said. "I see the need to consider skills, for expediency. Until the spring."

I finished reading the transcripts, marking the passages that did not agree. I rubbed my neck: my shoulders ached. I needed the baths, but that was not possible until later. Or maybe Druise would work the knots out with his strong fingers.

"*Princip*," I said, "I am doubtful that the Eastern Empire will send many troops, or officers, in the spring." I told him why.

"Turlo said the same." He exhaled, loudly. "Decanius is posturing, I believe. My fear is that he will convince Casil of the need, and what they will send will be the dregs of their army: bad soldiers and worse officers."

"Especially if Quintus wishes to show Eudekia that she was wrong in supporting us."

He looked up. "An interesting thought," he said. "You are thinking like a diplomat, Sorley."

I laughed. "Treachery is a frequent theme in the *danta*," I told him. I rolled the transcripts, tying them closed. "Not too much to argue over in the morning. Do you need me for anything else?"

"No. Are you going to see Cillian? I will come with you."

Gnaius was in the sickroom, bent over Cillian, probing the inflamed wounds. I thought he looked relieved to see me come in. Fear prickled. The physician straightened.

"I must open the wounds," he said. "There is infection, deep inside. The poultices have not been enough. I must drain it. It is the only chance, and it is very small." I went to Lena, putting an arm around her. Gnaius's grave tone had told her enough.

"Is he strong enough to survive this?" she asked,

her face white, when I had given her the news.

"He is certain to die, unless it is done." I touched Lena's belly with two fingers. "Do it," I urged. "For her, Lena. He swore he would leave no child fatherless. He would want to have the chance to keep that vow."

She nodded, slowly. "All right," she whispered. "When?" I asked.

"Now," Gnaius said. "I will give him poppy, and then I and Druisius will do what is needed. Everyone else must leave, Lord Sorley."

"A minute," Lena said. She turned back to the bed, to kiss Cillian gently. "*Thà mi gràh agäthe*," she murmured. She looked up. "Sorley?"

I took Cillian's hand. "Stay with us, *kärestan*," I whispered, and not caring if Druise was watching, bent to kiss his lips. Then I led Lena away.

She refused to go far, but Casyn convinced her to drink a little wine. "It will calm you," he said. "I must go, but you will send word. I am to be disturbed, regardless of what I am doing, and I will tell the door guard that."

A long time—or what felt like a long time—passed before Gnaius found us. "It is done," he said. "He is alive. Druisius is with him. I drained much poison and washed the wounds with wine and certain herbs. I will not sew them shut for a few days. But it may not be enough, you understand?"

I would not leave Lena's side, or Cillian's. "Tell Decanius I am ill, or whatever you need to," I said to Casyn, when he came himself to speak to me. "My first loyalty is here, *Princip*, and you knew that." He glanced down at Cillian, unmoving, breathing shallowly, then at Lena.

"Stay," he said. "Lena, I will petition the soldier's god, I promise. Sorley, a minute in the corridor?"

Outside the room, he faced me. "How long?"

"Gnaius will make no prognosis, either way," I told him. "There is still some fever, but he says the surgery may account for that. But if it worsens…"

"If Cillian dies," he said, "I have come to realize that the lives of all my people will change. Not just Lena's, and not just yours, Sorley." He sighed. "None of us can fight the battles of intellect and learning against Decanius that Cillian would be able to, and so we will have to submit to laws that I believe unjust, but that I have no defence against. Wars are not all fought with sword and bow. Send to me, if there is news."

Decanius, I was told, was furious at the delay. But while Michan was learning some of the language rapidly, he was not fluent enough to allow the talks to continue. I didn't really care. Cillian grew no better, and even I, who wanted to pretend it was not so, saw he could not live much longer. Every rib stood out, and the flesh of his face had fallen away, leaving the shape of the skull beneath starkly obvious. The hours by his side had become a death watch, for all I prayed—to any god who might listen—that it might be otherwise.

Lena never cried now, and rarely spoke to anyone except Cillian. She grew steadily thinner, drawn with exhaustion, but she sat holding his hand, dripping water into his mouth, rubbing salve into his hands and lips. I played, or took her place when she finally gave into fatigue, and Druise, grim and taciturn, made us both try to sleep for at least part of the night. Someone was always awake, our reason for that unspoken, but understood.

I was playing cradle tunes one afternoon—I was always playing cradle tunes, it seemed—when Talyn came in. "Sorley," she said, "You are needed. A man has arrived from Linrathe; sent by the Lady Dagney and the *Teannasach*, he says. Randall, his name is. The *Princip* asks if you could join them, for a short while."

"Go," Lena said. I hesitated.

"Half an hour," Talyn said. "If you would, Lord Sorley." I nodded, and stood, stiff from sitting. Handing my *ladhar* to Druise, I followed Talyn to Casyn's workroom. She touched my back as we walked; when I glanced at her, she shook her head, slowly, sadly.

"Randall na Asgaill." I greeted the man sitting with Casyn. I remembered him: younger than me, by several years, from a *torp* somewhere in the north of Linrathe. Not a *torpari*, but not a lord's son, either. My numbed mind refused to place him. Educated at the *Ti'ach na Asgaill*, where the focus was on mathematics, astronomy. How good was his Casilan?

"Lord Sorley." He stood, offering a hand.

"Forgive me, Randall, if I come to the point, but I have other duties," I said. "You were asked to come to Wall's End to teach Casilan to the officers here. Do not be offended, but I did not think it was much studied, at your *Ti'ach*."

"A common misunderstanding," he said. "It was, but perhaps with a different emphasis than at the *Ti'ach na Perras*. You learned to read the histories; we learned the mathematical texts, and some of the sciences." He smiled, his blue eyes crinkling. "But I assure you I know it well enough to teach the basics."

"You think you do," I said, and in Casilan, added, "but the spoken language does not sound the way we were taught." He frowned, and I repeated it, much more slowly. A faint comprehension rose on his face.

"Again?'

The third time, he answered me in a poor approximation of my pronunciation. "Closer," I said, reverting to our common language. "You will need some time to correct what you have learned. But it should not take you long. Reading it, of course, remains the same."

We arranged a time to meet. Birel appeared, to show Randall to his room, and explain meals and the baths. Casyn indicated I should stay.

"What do you know of him?"

I told him what I had recalled. "I can't remember just now who his father is, or which *torp* he is from. But that is easy to bring up, in conversation."

"Are you sure of his allegiance?"

"Not personally, no. But I cannot imagine Dagney would have agreed he should come, if she had doubts."

"How long before he can translate for us?" The rapid questions told me Casyn was worried about something.

"A few days, providing Decanius is reasonably patient with him. But that is not why he is here, *Princip*."

"It is not why he was sent. But if you believe he is trustworthy, it is what I need him to do, until you are free to return."

"But Lena will still need me, Casyn. I will not leave her to grieve alone."

"Nor will I ask you to, or diminish your own grief," he said. "But the Procurator demands a return to the talks. I have little choice but to use Randall."

"I can see that." I stood. "I will give him what time I can."

I ate with Randall that evening, although I had little appetite these days. Bluntly, to explain my preoccupation and lack of time, I explained about Cillian.

"I was told," he said. "A terrible loss. I knew him: he taught at my *Ti'ach* for a season, about six or seven years ago? It is in part why my Casilan is as good as it is. Or as I thought it was."

"We all thought that," I assured him. "Cillian was astounded at what we had forgotten, and changed, over the centuries."

"Tell me about Casil?" he asked.

"It is magnificent. But another time, Randall. What were you doing, before you were asked to come south?"

"Teaching, and some other work. My father is factor for the young *Teannasach's* great-uncle, Liam. I taught the children of Dun Ceànnar, and sometimes even Ruar himself, because he too had wished to learn Casilan."

"I am surprised they could spare you, then," I said. If he had been Ruar's teacher, I thought, he could be trusted. "But I am glad you are here. Shall we begin?"

After that first meal I refused to speak Linrathan to him. We met for the three meals of the day, and by the third day I deemed his pronunciation, and comprehension, adequate. He still had to think about some words, and his translation was slower than mine, but he would do. Winter approached, and there was much work to complete.

I took him to Casyn, after our evening meal, for a briefing on the courtesies and protocols when the Procurator was present, and the details of what his duties would be. It took a little time. Walking back to the infirmary, I could hear the wind outside; it had shifted, blowing hard off the sea. Rain lashed against shutters. I shivered in the unheated corridor, the torches guttering in the drafts.

A fire burned in Cillian's sickroom, with braziers set near the bed. I closed the door quickly to keep out the cold. Lena turned to me, her face pale.

"Touch him," she said, fear in her voice. I put a hand on his forehead.

"Dear gods," I said. Against my cold hand, his skin burned.

"He was warm, earlier, but I thought…" Her voice trailed off.

I wrenched the door open again. "Cadet!" I snapped. "Fetch the doctor." I heard running feet. Lena pulled the blankets down.

"Water," she said. I brought it, and a bowl and sponge. She began to bathe his face and neck. He did not move, his breath rasping. I felt the clench of fear at my heart, mixed with the dull acceptance of inevitability.

Gnaius came, Druisius with him. The physician felt Cillian's skin, took his pulse, listened to his heart. At his workbench, he mixed something, and carefully, using a tube, dripped it into Cillian's mouth. None of us spoke to him; his face was closed, concentrating. When the liquid was gone, he looked up.

"The fever has returned," he said. "He will die tonight, in the early hours."

"No," I whispered. Lena said nothing. She sat on the stool beside him, taking his hand. NO, I screamed silently. Blindly I picked up the *ladhar* to play the lullabies that soothed him. What else could I offer?

Hours passed. Gnaius fed Cillian more drugs. Druisius brought us soup, and wine, but it went untouched. Cillian's hands were cold, and his feet. I tried to rub warmth into them. I watched his chest rise and fall, and the flicker of movement under his closed eyelids. Druisius kept the fires burning. Gnaius sat, silently.

In the darkest part of the night I began to pace, grief and a desperate desire to do something warring inside me. "Cillian," I said, too loudly, "I faced down an Empress for you." My voice rose. "Must I now be Oraiáphon, and take my *ladhar* to the underworld to appeal to the god to give you back? I will, if I must." Druise got up. Without speaking he stopped my agonised movement, holding me tightly. He wouldn't have known what I said; I had spoken in Linrathan. With one arm he reached for the *ladhar*.

"Play," he said. "Better than shouting. Use your anger, *amané*. He may hear the music yet." I took the instrument. My fingers began *An dithës braithréan,* and this time Lena did not stop me. The notes of the lament for brothers separated forever by war rose into the dark. Did they fall, to charm the darkest god?

The night wore on. Gnaius still sat, watchful now, his eyes reflecting firelight. I went to Lena, wrapping my arms around her from behind. Her hand was on Cillian's; mine covered hers, my thumb tracing a line on his cold wrist. I rested my lips against her hair. Almost silently, she began to cry. "*Kärestan,*" she begged. "Please do not leave me. Do not leave us." The anguish in her voice was unbearable.

There was one thing I must do. Even as I went to the shutters I thought Cillian would have laughed at my superstition, but in Sorham and Linrathe, a dying spirit needed a window open, an escape. When the room was open to the night air—the rain had stopped, I half-noticed—I returned to his bedside. Gnaius watched what I did, but made no demur, perhaps understanding.

I took a deep breath. Nothing more now, except to ease his passing. I began to sing, a soothing tune, gentle. I put an arm around Lena, but my other hand stroked Cillian's forehead, and his hair. I wanted, fiercely, for him to feel himself a child again, safely falling asleep, secure and loved.

A dank smell, of wet soil and stone, of the depths of caves and dark places drifted into the room. I did not stop singing, sipping water when Druise insisted. My voice grew raw, hoarse, but still I sang. A shutter rattled on its hook, and the lamps guttered in a sudden warm breeze, carrying with it a faint scent of flowers. The sky beyond the window glowed pink in the first rays of the sun. Behind me, I heard Gnaius say something, low and incredulous.

Lena reached out to touch Cillian's face, still now and so pale. "Sorley," she whispered. I put my fingers beside hers. Cillian's skin was cool. Cool, but not cold.

"Gnaius?" I rasped. The physician placed his hand on Cillian's forehead, then took his wrist. Then he bent to place an ear to his chest and sniffed his skin. He straightened, raising an expressive eyebrow. "What god did you pray to?" he asked. "There is no fever, and his heart beats more strongly. He may yet live."

CHAPTER 7

DRUISE MADE GNAIUS give Lena and me poppy in wine, and we fell quickly into a drugged sleep, somehow sharing the narrow cot. I woke to the music of Linrathan lullabies, but they didn't quite sound right. Druise, I thought foggily, his *cithar*. If he's playing, then Cillian is still alive. I slipped off the cot, careful not to disturb Lena, and went to crouch beside him.

"No fever still," Druise whispered. "The gods intervened, I think, last night." He put his *cithar* down. "You will sit with him now? I will bring you some food."

"Yes. Thank you, Druise. For everything, last night, and for taking care of us. All of us."

"My job," he said briefly. He glanced down at Cillian. "A brave man," he said. "Maybe easier to die, than face what might be now."

I couldn't think about that. He was alive, and that was enough. "When," I said, attempting lightness, "did Cillian make the easier choice?"

"Not ever, that I know," Druise said seriously. "Soup, Sorley? Or something more?"

"Soup," I told him. "Get some sleep yourself, Druise. Has Casyn been told?"

"Yes. He will come, he said, when you are awake. I will let him know."

Casyn took a long look at Cillian, and at Lena, who still slept. Silently he motioned me to the corridor, sending the cadet to where she could not hear us.

"Gnaius says he will live?"

"May. He is a cautious man."

He nodded. "Keep me informed. Do not worry about leaving him. Your *consor*," he smiled, "is most adamant that you are needed here. An interesting man, Druisius. Respectful enough, but sure of his own worth. He reminds me in that way of Lena's father."

What had Druise said? "Thank you," I said. "How go the talks?"

"Randall's work is adequate. We move more slowly, perhaps, but that is not necessarily a bad thing. We are discussing weapons, and their manufacture. The Procurator wishes our troops to be taught the short sword, a necessity, he says. But we have very few, of course, and making more will take time. A different shield is needed, as well. The conversations are tedious, to say the least."

"And who will do the training?"

"Exactly. You can guess his suggestion. I wonder how many of his friends will arrive next summer?"

A messenger arrived from the south, with a letter for Decanius, and shortly after, he announced he must return to the Eastern Fort. He demanded a translator, one who could read, not just speak the language.

"I cannot go," I said to Casyn. "I cannot leave Lena, or Cillian."

"Druisius?"

"He cannot read your language." I didn't know if Druise could read at all. "Nor do I think Decanius would find him suitable, even if he could. He is a man conscious of rank and position." I didn't want Druise to go; Cillian needed him. So did I.

"Randall, then," he said. "Although he may refuse, and I have no power to compel him."

"What will Decanius be doing at the Eastern Fort?"

"He has not deigned to tell me," Casyn said, "but if he needs someone to read documents, then I would guess he wants to look at records. I wish I knew what his message said."

"Now there Druise might be useful," I said. "Is the messenger still here?"

"To the best of my knowledge, yes."

"I can ask," Druise said, "after enough wine. But he is unlikely to know."

"Try." I offered him some coins. "For better wine, or ale, or whatever he wants," I said.

"No," he said. "If I do that, he will suspect." He grinned. "You think this is the first time I have had such a task? I was not just a bedpet to my officers."

I went with him to check on Cillian. Lena was nearby, sewing and looking unhappy about it. "I hate this as much as my aunt Tali did," she said. "But this baby will need clothes."

"If neither Druise nor I are here this evening, will you be all right?" I asked. I explained why.

"Of course, providing someone comes to give Cillian his last dose of poppy."

"Gnaius, tonight," Druise said. "I will ensure it." To me, as we left the room, he added, "Do not wait up for me, Sorley. I will be late, and not sober."

"I may be little better," I said. Out of the building, he turned left, I right, towards the officers' commons. Wall's End had no provision for civilians; I ate mostly with Lena, or with Casyn if he required me to translate. If Randall was not with Decanius, he was most likely in the junior commons.

I found him sitting with a couple of young officers, ones whose names I could not bring to mind. He moved to a table with me without demur. We'd barely spoken since I'd given him his remedial instruction in spoken Casilan. The steward brought us wine.

"Have you eaten?" I asked Randall.

"Yes."

I requested food. When the steward had left us, I picked up my cup. "How is the work?"

"Not very interesting, if I am honest." He gave me a wry smile. "I am good with numbers, and the Procurator is pleased by that."

"Is that what you studied, at the *Ti'ach na Asgaill*?" I asked. The steward put a plate of stew in front of me, and some bread. I picked up my spoon. Mutton and barley, as familiar as the cries of seabirds.

"My *Mathàir* makes better," Randall said, indicating the plate, "but it was not bad. I studied mathematics, yes, and how to build structures using mathematical principles. But my *Athàir* taught me my numbers, and how to calculate, before I went there."

"As did mine," I said.

"Aye," he replied. "But a *Harr's* son learns so you can keep an eye on your factor's books."

"Is that what you think? You're as bad as Druisius. He doesn't believe I can shear sheep." I had made a mistake, and I knew it instantly. I had grown complacent, freely and familiarly speaking of Druise. But I had just equated Randall with my lover, reminding him of what I was, and perhaps insinuating he was the same. "I was overseeing the sales of those fleeces at sixteen," I went on, trying to make the conversation proceed naturally. "Things are likely different in the *Teannasach's* family, Randall, but on a Sorham estate, there is no factor. Believe me, we all worked."

"Plenty of time to make music, though, and the freedom to spend five years at a *Ti'ach* as a grown man."

A hard-won freedom, but I wasn't going to tell Randall that. "My father had a new wife," I said. "I think he was glad to have me gone, so he was not reminded he had an adult son waiting for him to die." I forced a grin. "And music stops us going mad in the winter, when there's nearly no light."

"Aye," he said, non-committal. "What did you want to see me about? It wasn't to reminisce about home, I have no doubt."

I told him of Decanius's demand. "The *Princip* will ask you formally tomorrow," I concluded, "but I thought you might want time to think about it. It is not what you were sent here to do."

He nodded. "I might go. I like the Procurator well enough, and I understand his job somewhat. He is but a factor in a larger way. It was good of you to mention it to me, Lord Sorley."

"I am not Lord Sorley to you, Randall," I said, not for the first time. The rules of the *Ti'acha*: no titles except the ones earned there, the right after five years of study to add the *Comiádh's* name to yours to tell the world who had taught you. I hadn't quite finished my requisite time, but under the circumstances, I thought it would be forgiven.

"Not easy to remember," he said. Inwardly I sighed. He was too conscious of his status, or lack of it. Was it harder for a factor's son, neither one thing nor the other, not a landholder but not quite a *torpari* either? Still, five years with Asgaill should have changed his perceptions. Really? I asked myself. Did all his time with Perras change Cillian's?

"It is a courtesy title," I reminded him. "The lands I were to inherit one day are in Marai hands now."

"But has not our *Teannasach* pledged to regain them? Might not these Casilani be useful in that?" He downed his wine before standing up. "I should ask: how is Cillian?"

"Still very ill," I told him, "but the physician says he will live."

"The Procurator was asking, you see." Was he? I tucked that piece of information away. Randall went back to the men he had been sitting with earlier. I sat, sipping the poor wine. *Might not these Casilani be useful?* Very possibly.

Druise woke me, coming in very late. The noise he made told me he was far from sober. "Tomorrow," he muttered, to my sleepy query. I fell asleep again to his rhythmic snoring.

Somehow, he roused himself at dawn, going to Cillian to administer the morning poppy. He came back a little later, to wake me again pouring water at the washstand.

"How's your head?" I asked from the bed.

He splashed about before answering. "Sore. I will live. At least I am not expected on the parade ground."

"Did you learn anything?"

"The letter is from a *mensore*, one whose responsibility was to identify sources of ore, iron and copper and lead. That is all. Except that the messenger hates it here, and wishes he had returned to Casil." He dried his face. "Your head is not sore."

"No. Randall preferred other company. But he told me he likes Decanius, which worries me." I sat up, yawning. "Casyn will be interested in what you learned, Druise. Thank you."

"Iron and copper and lead?" Casyn said. "There are maps, I remember, and records of yields. I knew more, once: it befitted a blacksmith to know where his metal came from."

"Who mines the ore?" I couldn't see women doing it.

"The army or retired officers, in the past, overseeing slaves and captives along the Durrains. But sometimes too the mines belong to a women's village, although only a few, and almost all copper deposits on headlands."

I discarded my presumptions. Women didn't take fishing boats out in Sorham, either. "There could be many reasons Decanius is interested. Did he not say all mines belong to the Empire? So he will want to claim the ones belonging to the villages."

"Likely. Perhaps not a bad thing, if there is not the labour to work them. We will need all the metals, with swords and shields to make. You say Randall will agree to go south?"

"I believe so. He likes Decanius, he says."

"Does he?" Casyn gave a mirthless chuckle. "I wonder why. However, that is one less thing I need to worry about. And I will welcome a break from these endless talks."

Cillian's skin remained cool, and his breathing no longer rasped. He was occasionally vocal, if incoherent, his eyes open but unseeing, and he moved more, too. Or had he just become very still in the days after the surgery, before the fever raged through him the second time?

"Be prepared," Gnaius told us. "He should return to us soon, but it may be with the mind of a small child. I cannot tell. The gods are capricious."

That will not happen, I told myself. Please not. That would be cruelty beyond comprehension. Better he had died. *Sometimes even to live is an act of bravery*, Catilius had written.

No, I said firmly,, but the thought would not go

away, although I could sometimes push it to the back of my mind. Lena and I had not spoken of what Gnaius had told us; she had held me, tightly, for a long moment afterwards, but that was all. She was so strong. I had to be, too.

I played a medley of lullabies and children's teaching songs, watching Lena bathe Cillian's face. She dried his skin gently, patting with a soft cloth, and began to salve his dry lips. He had been restless earlier, Druise had told me. "*Kärestan,*" she murmured, her finger spreading the balm along his lower lip, chapped and red. "Your daughter moved this morning, for the first time. Or maybe your son, but I think she's a girl." His eyelids flickered, as if in response to her words, and suddenly his eyes opened. I held my breath. He blinked, several times. Against the light? Hope surged, and with it, fear.

"Lena," he whispered, barely making the sounds. "*Käresta.*" I felt tears begin.

"Hello, my love," she murmured. "You have been asleep a long time. Let me give you some water." She dripped a spoonful between his lips, then another. His eyes never left her face. She kissed him, her lips barely brushing his. Behind me, I heard Druise leave the room.

I should leave them to each other, I thought.

Cillian closed his eyes, then opened them again. "Sorley?"

"He is here too." I put the *ladhar* down, unbelieving. Kneeling, I took his hand. His fingers grasped mine loosely.

"Music," he whispered. "*Meas.*"

Tears and laughter fought for ascendancy. "*Mo duíne gràhadh*," I replied. "I am so heartily tired of Linrathan cradle songs. Can I play something else now?"

CHAPTER 8

DRUISE HAD GONE FOR GNAIUS and Casyn, who arrived almost together. Casyn, pulled from talks with Decanius, wore the colours of office. The light was low in the room, but there was no mistaking the pale tunic, or the pendant.

"I am…sorry, *Princip*," Cillian murmured. Words took effort. He lay still. Lena gave him more water. "I didn't see," he managed.

"No more did Callan," Casyn said gently. "Do not worry, Cillian. There is no blame. We won. Fritjof is dead, and the Marai gone."

"Enough," Gnaius said firmly.

"Linrathe?" Cillian whispered.

"Is safe. Ruar is at Dun Ceànnar," I answered. "All is well, *mo charaidh*."

"You will all leave, please," Gnaius said. "Except Druisius. Wait in the corridor."

"He knows us," Lena said, leaning against me. She

was allowing herself to cry now, tears of relief and fear assuaged. I wrapped my arms tighter around her, rocking her a little. My own eyes were still wet.

"More than that," Casyn said. "To understand so quickly what I wear means…remarkable."

Gnaius came out of the sickroom, closing the door quietly. "You must listen," he began. "He is sleeping. He will sleep and wake and sleep again, for many days. His mind, from what I saw, appears undamaged. But his body? There is much inflammation, and until that subsides, I cannot know how much permanent damage has been done.

"His pain is intense. He will need poppy syrup for many weeks. He is too weak to withstand the pain without it; he would not be able to sleep, and without sleep he will succumb again to fever. This is a long recovery, you understand? Many months, and it may never be complete."

Lena frowned, looking worried. "He hates drugs," she said. "He would barely accept willow-bark, before. He will argue against the poppy syrup." The physician shook his head.

"He must take it," he said. "I will explain, if he begins to baulk. He must be kept quiet, too. His *quincala*, of course, and you, Lord Sorley, for the music which so soothes him, but even the two of you should not be together, when he is awake. One other person, for a minute or two, each day, perhaps." He cleared his throat. "I believed he would die. It is not my skill that has saved him, but the gods. For what reason, I do not know."

Lena slept, deeply, curled on the cot in the sickroom. I returned to the stool beside Cillian, not playing, just sitting. Thinking, about many things. Cillian moaned slightly, moving his head. He opened his eyes.

"*Mo duíne gràhadh*," I said softly. "Lena is sleeping." Druise wasn't in the room. I bent to kiss him, allowing myself the gesture, the affirmation.

He smiled, just a brief curve of his lips. I gave him a little water.

"When?" he asked.

"Five weeks to midwinter," I said. "We are at Wall's End."

"Casil?"

"Casil?" I repeated, puzzled. "They came, yes." Did he not remember?

"No. The treaty."

"There are talks. I translate for Casyn. They go well enough." Not quite the truth, but all he needed to know. He smiled again and drifted back into sleep. I picked up his hand, stroking his fingers. His nails needed cutting. I could do that, I thought, and went to Gnaius's worktable to find clippers. Cillian did not wake while I trimmed his fingernails. I watched him sleep, hearing Lena's regular breathing from the cot behind me.

I had a responsibility now. To Cillian and to Lena,

and the unborn child, and perhaps to Druisius as well. I must try to be, for an unknown time, what Cillian had been among the four of us: the guiding presence, the leader. I am taking on his roles, I thought. The idea made me uncomfortable, as if I were usurping him, somehow. But not forever, I told myself. He will recover. He must.

I heard Cillian's scream of pain from the hallway. I started to run, but the cadet stepped in front of the door. "No entry," he said. "My orders, Lord Sorley."

Lena appeared from further down the corridor. "Gnaius and Druise are with him. They are moving his leg; Gnaius says it is necessary. They told me to go away."

Another scream. She winced. I put my arms around her. The cadet's face was crumpled, the boy barely controlling himself. "Then we should," I said. "We have to trust Gnaius. Come."

I took her back to the room I had claimed as a workroom. She shook her head at the offer of wine, so I added wood to the fire and made tea instead.

"How are the talks?" she asked, her hands wrapped around the cup.

"Decanius has broken them off until he returns from the south," I reminded her. "He leaves in a few days. Casyn and his advisors are working on the reorganization of the army. Which cohorts to keep, and which to combine, and who might be promoted. That sort of thing. I'm not involved."

She sipped the tea. "I wonder if Casyn would let me help."

"Do you want to?"

"I have to do something, at least for part of the day. Druise—" She took a breath. "He will say this to you too. He said when they are doing these exercises in the mornings, and at night, Cillian needs to be free to scream or cry, and if he thinks you or I are near, he won't."

I swore. "Catilius," I said, "has a lot to answer for." She nodded, smiling a little.

"My thought too. But Druise is right, isn't he? They will dose him with poppy after, so he will sleep. I must be there when he is awake, afterwards, or you, but in the mornings at least I need employment. I am," she added, "still a lieutenant, after all."

"On leave," I said, "officially." I wondered if Casyn would let her be part of the talks; she hadn't the necessary rank to advise him. "And you need to rest, Lena. You're recovering too, in a different way, and you're pregnant."

"I know," she said. "I get tired easily. But I can sleep all night now, and sitting with Cillian is no longer a strain. And as for being pregnant, Sorley, when has that ever stopped a woman from working?"

I laughed. "Not at Gundarstorp," I admitted.

"Nor at Tirvan. I will talk to Casyn. What about you? What will you do?"

What could I do? I searched my mind. When the answer came to me, it was so obvious I wondered just how tired I was too, not to have seen it sooner. "What Randall was meant to," I said. "Teach the officers Casilan."

We talked for a while longer, about the changes Decanius was demanding, about Druise's surprising competency as a nurse, about the name—Gwenna—that Lena was considering for the baby. "For my mother, and his," she told me. "Gwen and Hafwen, but his father called her Wenna."

"And if it's a boy?"

"Colm. If Cillian agrees, of course," she added.

"Have you told him?"

"Not yet. I will, soon. When he's a little stronger."

"Wouldn't knowing buoy him?" I asked. "Give him something to look forward to?"

"Perhaps." She put down her cup. "Or something to worry about. This baby is a possible heir to the title of *Princip*, and I do not want the implications of that concerning him yet."

"I thought Cillian renounced his right to inherit," I said.

"He did, for himself. We did not believe we had the right to make that choice for our children, although for Cillian that was only an intellectual decision. I wonder now if he would have felt the same, had he known of her." She touched her belly, only slightly swollen. "But that cannot be changed." She stood. "Nor can certain effects of pregnancy. The tea was welcome, but I had better leave you now."

How did you teach a language? I tried to remember what Perras had done, but it didn't help: he had been primarily teaching us to read Casilan, not speak it, and speaking was the priority here. I had come to the *Ti'ach* fluent in Marái'sta, having learned it from earliest childhood. How had Dagney taught me the language of the Western—or Southern, as we had called it— Empire? In the classroom, I remembered: basic vocabulary, the phrasing of common sentences. But then at meals, and while playing music, or just in simple requests. I'd have to mimic that, as best I could. And what, in the interactions between officers and men, and officers and Casilani officers, were the words they needed to know?

I asked Druise that night, when he'd finally come to our room. He smelt of beer, and he wasn't quite sober. "I will write you a list," he said, "tomorrow." A question answered, I thought: if he can write, he can read. "Time to sleep now." He sounded tired, and out of sorts.

"What's wrong?" I asked.

He grunted. I ran my hand over his back. "Druise?"

"Mostly I like my work," he said. "Not this part."

"Which part?"

"The exercises. Cillian screaming. It is hard." I rubbed his neck, feeling the tension there.

"Can't you ask Gnaius to use one of the medics to help?"

"No. Cillian is my officer. There will be enough talk, from the cadets on the door. He does not need others to hear, or see his tears."

"Music wouldn't help? I could—"

"No. After, yes, when he has had the poppy. Enough, *amané*. I need to sleep, and I do not want talk of Cillian in our bed."

I couldn't argue with that; it was only fair, and he'd said it gently. "There won't be," I said. "I promise."

"Linrathan men," he said. "Everything a promise." He stood, wearily. "Better not to make them. They tempt the gods."

He stripped off his clothes and lay down, pulling the blankets over him. He'd be asleep in seconds, I knew. "Druise?" He muttered my name. "You said it's better to use anger. Can't I—can't we—?"

He opened one eye. "Tonight, no. But yes. If you want."

Even his words aroused me. "I want," I said, hoarsely. He flashed a sleepy grin.

"Good. Tomorrow."

⌗

"Get out of my way, girl!" Angry words, spoken in a heavily accented voice. Druise swore and began to run. I followed. At the door to the infirmary, Phaulius, Decanius's aide, pushed the cadet aside. He reached for the handle, just as Druise's big fist smashed upward into his jaw.

The man stumbled, recoiling off the stone wall. Druise grabbed him, wrenching both arms behind his back. "His knife," he ordered. I pulled Phaulius's knife from his belt, avoiding a kick. The man was a head taller than Druise, but nowhere near as strong.

"You all right?" Druise said to the cadet. She nodded. "Then go for help." He pushed Phaulius up against the wall, face forward. Blood was dripping onto the flagstones. I undid my belt and wound it around the man's wrists, and by the time other guards arrived he was on his knees, Druise's foot on one ankle, breathing in gasps and snuffles.

"What happened?" the senior of the two guards asked. Druise told him, succinctly. He turned to the cadet, who confirmed what Druise had said. "And you, Lord Sorley?"

"Exactly what you have heard," I said. "I have his belt knife; I took it from him after Druisius had restrained him. And I'd like my belt back, please."

"Wait," Druise said to them. He went into the infirmary, returning with small pieces of cloth. He twisted them, pushing one into each of Phaulius's nostrils. The man gasped, trying to jerk his head away, but Druise had a hand firmly on his jaw. "Stop him trailing blood all down the halls," he said. One of the guards grinned.

"Come on, Phaulius, it's the cells for you." They helped him up, none too gently. "What sort of idiot are you? The cadet's orders come from the physician Gnaius, and he outranks you."

"He doesn't outrank the Procurator," Phaulius said thickly. He spat blood.

"Did you tell her that?"

"She should have known who I was."

"Would that have been enough in Casil? And I thought we were being told how superior your discipline is to ours. Get moving." The second guard led him away. The *capora* turned to the girl. "Well done, Cadet. Now get the floor washed." He held out a hand to me. "I'll take the knife. You'll get your belt back."

"What did he say to you?" Druise asked the cadet, when the guard had left.

"He wanted to see Major Cillian."

"That was all?"

"Yes, sir. I said he could not, that I had no orders to allow him. I was polite, sir."

"And you are not hurt?"

"No, sir."

Druise grinned. "Then do as the *capora* ordered and wash the floor. The Major will be safe. I will be with him, and Lord Sorley with me."

⌗

Unsurprisingly, the next day we were called to Casyn's workroom, to face a furious Procurator. Phaulius was not present.

"Who is this soldier?" Decanius demanded. "He attacked my aide."

"My guards report your aide was assaulting a cadet following her orders," Casyn said. "Druisius did what I would expect any soldier in my army to do, and defended her."

"Phaulius was there as my representative, enquiring as to the health of the Emperor's son. The girl had no right to deny him entry to the infirmary."

"The cadet," Casyn emphasized the rank, "had every right. The Major's physician has been specific about who may see him. Even I must request permission to have someone accompany me, Procurator, and the Major is my nephew, I will remind you."

Decanius glared at Casyn, his balding head gleaming red. "Druisius, you say? That is not a name from this land."

"No," Casyn said. "Druisius joined my army, Procurator, after the Taiva, with several other men from Casil who had a liking for this land. He is Major Cillian's soldier-servant."

"Who was your commander?" Decanius snapped at Druisius.

Druise waited for Casyn's nod before he answered. Decanius frowned. "And why did you stay?"

"I like adventure, Procurator." Decanius studied him, eyes narrowed. Druise stared at the wall.

"Why does your nephew have a Casilani soldier-servant?" At the *Princip's* hesitation, Druise answered.

"I have skills in nursing, Procurator. Learned when I was assigned to an injured officer in Casil."

"I see. *Princip*, I am displeased. This man should be punished."

"Punished?" Casyn said coldly. "For protecting the officer to whom he is assigned? I think not, Procurator. Ensure your aide follows protocol in the future, and I will seek no further punishment for him, for his mistreatment of a cadet. Are we agreed?"

"It will do," Decanius said, after a moment.

"Good," Casyn said. "And as you were so determined to discover, Procurator, my nephew is expected now to live, although his recovery will be long and difficult."

"So we will not see him at our discussions? Not even when I return from the south?"

"It is unlikely, unless you are gone for many weeks."

"A regret," the Procurator said, but I was sure he meant the opposite.

"Sit, Druisius," the Princip said, once Decanius had left. I, as the translator, had already been seated. "What did you make of that? Sorley?"

"It seemed too easy. Unless he knows Phaulius is at fault."

"He is at fault. Regardless, it is out of character for Decanius, in my experience. Do you have any other thoughts?"

"Perhaps one." I paused, trying to think of a way to explain. "You know I am a musician. I sing only adequately, but I can hear when a voice is being constrained by fear or tension. There is a tightness in the expression. Every time Decanius has spoken of Cillian, I have heard that tightness."

"Interesting. You think he is afraid of Cillian?"

"Afraid of what he can do in negotiations, given what his uncle, Quintus, might have told him?"

"Was Phaulius searched?" Druisius asked.

"Not that I know of. What are you thinking?"

"Poison. Easy enough to put in a water flask." He sounded very sure of that.

Casyn leaned back in his chair, arms crossed. "Are you speaking from experience, Druisius? Don't answer that," he added. "A cadet is not a sufficient guard, then. I will assign soldiers, day and night. From our own troops. Druisius, thank you. Lord Sorley, please stay."

"Do you think Decanius would seriously try to poison Cillian?" I asked. Even for the Procurator, that would be extreme. Casyn tapped his fingers on the table.

"I think it is possible. Decanius knows I have not the knowledge to counter his arguments, nor always the skill. The man I knew Cillian to be would. If, as I pray, his mind is undamaged by his illness and the drugs he must take, and he recovers in time, we might salvage some rights to our own traditions and laws. Without Cillian, I have no doubt we will be subsumed into the ways of the Eastern Empire."

He had spoken starkly; not resigned, quite, but a man telling an unpalatable truth.

"Turlo could not help?" I asked.

"I doubt it, Sorley," he said. "I feel like a man trying to hold back the tide, knowing it will sweep over us no matter what I do."

Gnaius had told Lena to go out into the fresh air, good for her and the baby, he said. Mostly she went alone: mornings, when Cillian's treatments and exercises occurred, conflicted with my teaching and the duties Casyn had found for her. Officially, she transcribed, suitable work for a junior officer. But some days we were both free to walk down to the harbour, or ride along the road that ran beside the Wall, talking usually of little things. On this cloudy, cool morning, we'd chosen to ride. Perhaps half-way to the first guardpost east of Wall's End,

Lena pointed ahead. "Riders."

The distance between us lessened. Sun broke free of the clouds, shining on the right-hand rider's red hair. "Turlo!" Lena urged her horse forward into a canter. I kicked my gelding's flanks and followed.

She slid off the horse and into Turlo's outstretched arms. He hugged her, hard, then stepped back a little, looking at her face, and mine. "There is good news?"

"Yes," Lena said. "He is awake, and alert. In much pain, but he will live."

"Oh, lassie," Turlo said, enveloping her again in his arms. "I barely dared ask. But seeing you smiling—" He looked up at the other man. "Get off that horse, Galen, and greet your daughter."

Galen dismounted, offering Lena the soldier's embrace. "You have done great things, I am told," he said.

"What I was trained for."

"Killing Fritjof, yes," he replied. "But crossing the Durrains, and beyond?"

"I brought him," Turlo said, "so you can tell him exactly what you did. He keeps asking and I cannot supply the details." He sounded amused, a friend indulging another's fancy.

"It could be useful to know," Galen said. He turned to me. "Lord Sorley."

"It is good to see you again, Galen."

"At least this time I am not taking you prisoner."

He grinned, remembering, and so did I.

"Why are we standing here?" Turlo asked. "I've a friend to see." He put a hand on Lena's arm. "Lassie, may I say...I feared for the child, in your anguish. I am glad to see I need not have worried."

Lena smiled. "She is strong, this one. But, Turlo, Cillian does not know. Do not mention it."

It puzzled me that Lena had still not told Cillian and that he had not noticed. Her belly had only begun to visibly swell in the past week or two, and without the strong breeze pushing her tunic tight, I doubted Turlo would have been sure. But she would have to tell Cillian soon.

"Turlo," I asked, as we rode west, "when were you at Dun Ceànnar last? I wrote to Ruar, telling him Cillian would live, more than two weeks ago."

"We'd left by then," Turlo said. "We rode east, to the track below the Durrains, and came south that way."

"Why?"

"I had an idea that if any of Fritjof's men had escaped, they might go east again."

"And attack over the Durrains?" Lena asked. "I doubt it, Turlo. It took us months to cross them on foot. To bring an army, pack animals, equipment? No."

"I wish there was a map," Galen said.

"There is," I said. "I've seen it."

"So has Cillian," Lena remembered. "He alluded to it once, and an older one. He said they didn't agree on how wide the mountains were."

"Where is this map?" Turlo demanded.

"At the *Ti'ach*. I can have it sent, I would think," I answered. "Maybe now you've crossed them, Lena, the map will make sense to you?"

"Maybe," she said. "Maybe to Cillian, too. He kept notes, the entire journey. But I don't know where his books are."

"I will wager, lassie," Turlo said, "that Birel has them."

Lena grinned, her face alight in a way I had not seen in so very long. "Would you now?" she said. "And what are you prepared to bet, General?"

Turlo sighed in relief when I told him Decanius was in the south. "Officious man," he muttered. We rode into the fort, leaving the horses at the stables. Galen and Turlo spoke quietly for a moment before Galen left us, heading to the soldiers' commons for the midday meal.

"When can I see Cillian?" Turlo asked.

"Late afternoon," Lena told him. "He will not be awake until then. And only for ten minutes."

"Understood," he said. "I'd best report to Casyn." He strode off, then turned on his heel. "I almost forgot. I've a letter for you, Sorley, from Dun Ceànnar. It's in my saddlebags. Where will you be, later?"

"Teaching," I said, "for most of the afternoon. With Lena in the infirmary, after that."

"I'll send a cadet with it." Lena watched Turlo for a moment, smiling.

"He cheers you up," I observed.

"I've always liked him," she said. "But it's the first time I've told anyone Cillian will live; anyone who wasn't here, I mean. It made it real, somehow."

I gave her a quick hug. "Shall we eat?" As we walked towards the junior officers' commons, I remembered my earlier confusion. "Lena, why have you still not told Cillian about the baby? He is stronger, and you can't put it off much longer."

"Because there are complications I cannot solve."

I frowned. "What complications, Lena?"

"For all Cillian's oath to this Empire, Sorley, he is Linrathan. The night before the Taiva, we talked about where home was, after. Home for all of us, including you; he was very clear on that, you know. You had to be there too. There is only one place that can be that home, isn't there? The *Ti'ach*?"

"In what could have been your last hour together, he was thinking of me?"

"Of course he was," Lena said, a bit impatiently. "Sorley, love and responsibility are inseparable in Cillian's mind. You know his vow to me, that he will shelter me all my life. He has not told me what he has vowed regarding you, but since he wants you with him always, it will be something similar."

"Wants me with him always?" I repeated. Words I had dreamed of hearing for almost a decade.

"Have you not realized that yet?" Lena said. "I

need your help, Sorley. If we are to go home to Linrathe, this child must be legitimate. We need to marry, but I don't know how to go about it. Marriage does not exist, in this land. Who can perform the ceremony, in Linrathe?"

"*Scáeli'en*," I said, "or at least, those who are senior enough. After seven years, I think. Not that it matters. Dagney is the senior *scáeli* of Linrathe, in rank if not in years. And there is no one else who should preside over Cillian's marriage."

Lena laughed, delighted. "No one else indeed," she said. "She will be pleased, won't she?"

"Very," I assured her.

"Then I can tell him now," she said. "Thank you. He'll be awake, I think. I'll eat later."

I stared after her. Go home to Linrathe. Lena was letting herself think of the future again, a future with Cillian—and me. Unexpected anger, sudden and intense, flared. Cillian would recover, and I would be caught between him and Druisius, loving the man I could not have; not loving the man I should. If he had told me what he had told Lena before the Taiva, that he wanted me by his side, wanted me at the *Ti'ach* with him...maybe I wouldn't have asked Druise to be my partner. Because, of course, Druise was a soldier. He couldn't just come to Linrathe, and we couldn't be lovers there anyway.

I swore. At the gods. At fate. At Cillian. My stomach clenched, bile rising in my throat. Grow up,

I told myself. You can't be angry.

Not at him.

I was walking down the corridor after teaching, still chatting to the officer with me in Casilan, when a cadet brought me the letter. I read it quickly, swearing softly. I was summoned to Dun Ceànnar, to be formally made *toscaire* to the Western Empire, and I needed to be there for midwinter, which was not all that far away. I would be gone several weeks, perhaps a little longer, and I didn't want to go. But I had little choice. My country's leader had given me an order I was bound to obey.

I entered the infirmary room quietly, thinking Cillian might still be sleeping. He was, and so was Lena, on the cot near his bed, but my entrance woke her. She yawned. "I was only dozing. But I'll leave him with you. He was awake, earlier, so he might sleep longer than usual." She stopped to watch him for a moment before she left. I sat by Cillian's bedside, thinking about riding north, and what I might expect at Dun Ceànnar.

Cillian woke an hour later. Druise, knowing the schedule, appeared, to wash and reposition him. I played, sitting under the window: I still didn't like watching this. Druise made Cillian as comfortable as possible, before coming over to me. "Do not stay long," he said quietly.

When he'd left, I put the *ladhar* down. "How are you?" I asked Cillian.

"Overwhelmed," he said. His voice was stronger, but there was a note of something new this afternoon. Disbelief? Wonder?

"Why, *mo charaidh*?"

He pushed himself up just slightly and smiled, a brilliant, joyous smile that lit his thin face. "You knew, of course, but I did not, until earlier today."

"Lena told you about the child," I said, smiling. "Is it not the best news, Cillian?" My earlier anger had dissolved. Druise and I—well, it had never been serious, had it?

"Not ever an expectation, in my life," he said softly. "But nor was Lena. Sorley," he added, seriously, "you will take care of her—of them—if I die?"

"You won't," I told him, "but of course, *mo duíne gràhadh*. As if you had been born my brother. I promise."

"*Meas*," he murmured. "How long to the spring equinox?"

"Midwinter is in two weeks, so, just over three months."

"Not long," he said thoughtfully. "I would like to be free of the poppy, when the child is born."

"Gnaius must guide you in that," I said. "Are you strong enough for other news?"

"I think so. Is it bad?"

"Not very. Only that I will be gone, for a month or so, over midwinter."

He took this in. "Why?"

"You may find this amusing," I told him. "I am Linrathe's new *toscaire* to the Empire, as of midwinter, by Ruar's bidding, and his great-uncle's approval. I must ride to Dun Ceànnar for my instructions."

"I wish you joy of Liam," he said. "A reward for your service, but one that keeps you a safe distance from Ruar?"

"How can you do that?" I demanded, smiling. He had sounded almost like himself. "Even drugged and in pain, you are more perceptive than I."

"Long practice," he replied, with an echo of a grin. "And the pain is not so bad, just now. Will you go to the *Ti'ach*?"

"On my way back." I would tell him of Perras's death when I returned.

"Good. They will be relieved to see you." He frowned. "When do you leave?"

"The day after tomorrow."

"Then perhaps I can write a letter, before you go. There is nothing wrong with my hands."

"I will send it from Heurlstorp. I won't make them wait several more weeks to hear from you," I said.

Lena returned, her hair damp. She'd been at the baths, I realized. I gave her a hug. "He is very happy," I murmured.

"Yes," she said. "Unbelieving at first, but the evidence," she touched her belly, "cannot be denied." She sat down beside the bed. "Our daughter was kind enough earlier to kick several times, so that her father could feel her move." Cillian reached for her hand, his long fingers tangling in hers. She bent to kiss him, not the brief brush of her lips from the weeks of vigil, but a longer kiss. Her free hand cupped his cheek. A rush of emotions caught me unawares: joy, hope, and envy mixed together, but stronger than those, overwhelming relief, and gratitude.

Before this last year I had only ever desperately wanted two things: to be a *scáeli*, and Cillian. The first would never happen now: it required years of travel and song-gathering. I had dreamt, once, of riding by his side as he travelled, he the *toscaire*, I the musician. But...*he wants you with him always.* We would still be together. There is very little I would not do, I thought, for this privilege.

CHAPTER 9

HEAVY GREY CLOUDS HUNG over the hills, the horizon blending into the sky. Snow, I thought, at least on higher ground. The vagaries of Linrathe's weather meant I had needed to leave well in advance of mid-winter: I could find myself snowed in at any point in the ride. I would travel from *torp* to *torp*, hospitality automatically offered to any traveller, but especially to someone who was both a *toscaire* and a musician. And a lord, truth be told. I would have the best bed available, and the best food, and someone else would rub down and feed my horse and clean my tack and boots. I wondered how Cillian, ascetic and self-sufficient, had dealt with all that. He had probably refused most of it, I thought, accepting only what etiquette required. I couldn't remember, from the few days he had stayed with us when I was sixteen.

I rode east, along the Wall's road. There was no defined track in Linrathe between Wall's End and the road from the Wall to the Sterre, and with snow threatening I would not risk riding cross-country. I wore a fur-lined cloak, slung open over a woollen tunic and breeches, and there were matching gloves and a cap in my saddlebags. I didn't need them, yet. An identical cloak, and gloves, would be delivered to Druisius on Midwinter's Day, my present to him.

Druise. I thought about the previous night; my increased confidence, his deep, delighted laughter. I touched my shoulder, just where it met my neck. I'd need to keep my shirts laced, or explain the bite marks.

Cillian wants you with him, always, Lena had said. Could I have a life that was both with him and not with him? I didn't feel bereft because he loved Lena, but wasn't that because of Druise? Who I was with him was someone Cillian didn't know, or Lena. I barely did myself, in truth, but I was learning.

What would Cillian think? I didn't know, and I didn't think I cared. The idea irritated me, somehow. What he and Lena shared wasn't for me to know, and neither did he have any right to know what my relationship with Druise entailed.

But you always had a life without him, my mind said. Music.

A solitary life, I argued, but no longer. I can make music with Druise; we have that, too. Music and bed, in Druise's words, and much to learn about both. Something separate and private, not crossing into Cillian and Lena's life together. Which was fine, at Wall's End, but what would happen when it was time to return to the *Ti'ach*?

Write some songs, I told myself. Truth could be found in wine, but for me, it was also found in the melodies and the words that flowed when my fingers touched the strings of my *ladhar*. Music would give me answers.

At every *torp* where I stopped, I was questioned about Cillian. Somehow, the news of his injuries and illness had spread across Linrathe. I reassured the *Eirënnen* and their wives, and I saw nothing but relief from them all. A tear or two from a *Konë*, and a surprising gentleness from her husband, at one *torp*. "She was fond of him," he said to me gruffly, later, "and what harm was there in it? We all knew what was said."

I'd heard the stories too, and Lena had told me they were true. That Cillian had vowed never to father a child because he had been fatherless himself—but the beds of women were another source of information and opinion. So he had given—and taken, no doubt—pleasure without risking conception. "I became adept at holding a civilized conversation with an *Eirën*, after I had spent part of the previous night with his wife," he'd said to me once, his voice reflecting his revulsion at what he'd done. He'd turned away from that life the year I'd come to the *Ti'ach,* resigning his position as *toscaire.*

I brought the talk around to Ruar and his great-uncle. From every *Eirën,* I heard respect for Liam, if not always liking. By the time I rode into Dun Ceànnar's long valley, I had a picture of a cautious, conservative man, but one who was loyal to Linrathe, its customs and its people.

Alone among the estates of Linrathe, Dun Ceànnar was more stronghold than *torp,* the associated village sitting some half-mile down its valley, with the massive stone house commanding a position on the hillside. Attack from above was just about impossible, and its long view down the glen meant invaders would be seen early in their approach. Ruar's family had been the leaders of Linrathe for more generations than I could remember, and their importance was reflected in the house's construction and position.

Men waited for me outside the house as I rode up the track. I was expected, and I rode bareheaded and with my cloak swept back, revealing that I carried no sword. I tolerated the assessing gazes. Well, I thought, I am fair-haired. But would any Marai approach the house so brazenly?

"My lord Sorley," one of the men said when I was close enough. "I will take your horse to the stables. Please go with my companion."

I dismounted and began to unfasten my saddlebags. "I can do that, my lord," the first guard said. "I will bring them to your room."

"You will forgive me," I said firmly, "but as you may know I am a musician, and no musician will trust his instrument to another man, however well-meaning. I will take my bags."

"As you wish," he said. He led my horse away, and I followed the second guard up the steps and into the house. I stopped inside the door, letting my eyes adjust to the dimness. Stone flags on the floor; stone walls, high rafters: this would have been the original hall, back when this was just another *Eirën's* house, a long structure of hall and ancillary rooms. It was little different, if a bit larger, than the hall at the *Ti'ach*. But as the family's importance had grown, so had the house, and now this was just a space between the outdoors and the fastnesses beyond.

I shed my cloak, hanging it on a peg on the wall, and let the guard guide me along a passage and to a closed door. He knocked, and at a word from inside, opened the door. "The Lord Sorley," he announced.

I stepped inside. Ruar was on his feet, a smile of welcome on his face; his great-uncle Liam did not rise, nor smile. The guard closed the door. "Sorley!" Ruar said. "I hoped you might come today. Was it a difficult ride? Would you like refreshment?"

"Ruar," I acknowledged him. "You look well. As do you, *Raséair*," I added, turning to Liam.

"I am well enough," Liam grunted. We exchanged the necessary pleasantries, and a brief description of my travels north. Tea and oatcakes were brought. Ruar might be the *Teannas'óg*, but he was also a growing boy, and most of the oatcakes went to him.

Liam finished his tea. "We'd best do the oath," he said, "so that we can talk of what we expect of you, Sorley. A few questions, first."

"Before that," Ruar said, interrupting his great-uncle, "tell me how Cillian does. He lives? The General Turlo told us it was unlikely."

"He does," I told him, "although it was not expected. He is awake now, but still very weak, and in much pain. He sends his greetings to you both."

"I am glad to hear it," Ruar said. "I liked Cillian, when I met him at the Eastern Fort. He explained the treaty and what it meant for Linrathe and my people extremely well. I would have liked more opportunity to learn from him."

"We will think more of your schooling in the spring," Liam said. "To our business, now. Before you swear this oath, there are questions I must ask. Questions that should have been asked before, and not just of a boy not affirmed by his family to succeed."

"It was Ruar's name the men of Linrathe rallied around," I said. "Perhaps not affirmed by his family, but chosen by his people, surely? In their eyes, and from what I heard on the road, he is *Teannasach* already."

"Yes," Liam said, "and we have accepted their choice. It would be unwise on our part to ignore it, after Lorcann. But he is not *Teannasach* yet, and as his regent I will have questions and challenges from the *Eirënnen* who advise us, and I must be able to answer."

I had expected this. Even at the *torps*, there had been some talk of the treaty, and how it had been decided, and not everyone had been pleased that a distant, foreign Empress now had influence over Linrathe. But the details were not known, nor my role in it, and I had pleaded that I had no right to speak of it as *toscaire* until my appointment had been confirmed. But if there was a council of the *Teannasach's* advisors in the spring, as traditionally there was, Liam—and perhaps Ruar—would indeed face some hard questions.

"Please ask what you need to," I said. I glanced at Ruar. He sat quietly, slightly frowning, but in concentration, I thought. He looked a bit like his father.

"Then answer me this," Liam said, and his voice was suddenly colder, "what right had you to give away the independence of Linrathe? Deciding our country's fate is the prerogative of its people. Even the *Teannasach* is responsible to them."

"I was as much the voice of our people as anyone, *Raséair*. My instructions came from Perras, who had long advised Donnalch and knew his mind. I left a country on the edge of defeat and found a chance for support against the Marai. I took it, after much long thought and deliberation." My argument sounded weak to my own ears. I was not Cillian, trained to the precision of diplomatic talks.

I was a musician, and I had wanted to be a *scáeli*. "*Raséair*, my own lands are forfeit." I dropped my voice, slowing my speech. "I have lost the sound of waves on the sea-coast, and the fog lying low over the water, and the barking of seals on the shingle. I have lost the eagle above the mountains, and the purple of the heather on the hill, and the grave of my mother. All those I gave willingly. Perhaps I had no authority, except that of love for Linrathe, to see it not subject to Fritjof's brutality." I paused. "But what would you have done, in my place?"

Silence. Liam studied me, thoughtfully. "I may recall you, in the spring, to say those words again to the council," he said finally. "If the *scáeli* plays *An dithës braithréan* quietly as you speak, you will have them in the palm of your hand. You have a brother, do you not?"

"I do," I said. "Two, actually. Roghan is three years younger than I. The little one, who is a half-brother, I have never met; he is five." He nodded.

"And what of the fact that the treaty was negotiated by agents of the southern Empire, and not by you at all? You agreed to terms, nothing more."

"Cillian na Perras negotiated the terms for

Linrathe. Sworn to his father's country he may now be, and nearly gave his life for it, but compare the treaties, *Raséair.* The southern Empire is now no more; Casyn is not the Emperor, nor will there be another. Their laws are now Casil's laws, and Casil's Empress theirs. Ruar will be *Teannasach,* and our laws and independence are mostly untouched. There is tribute to pay, admittedly, but we were paying Varsland, before. Is this a treaty negotiated by a man who does not love the land of his birth?"

"But one who Donnalch never trusted," Liam said bluntly.

"Donnalch was mistaken in that," I answered firmly.

"I agree," Ruar said. "My father was a wise man, and his judgement fair and thoughtful, but in this he was wrong, great-uncle."

"Perhaps," Liam said. "You do not know all of it. Now, Sorley, there is an oath to be sworn, and for that we must be outside. You have a cloak? And after that is done, will you explain to Ruar exactly what you just did here, how you used words and the pitch and tone of your voice to convince? A *scáeli's* trick, and you did it well. Ruar, you must learn to recognize this, and guard against it."

We went out, into the thin sunshine, and across the cobbles of the forecourt. When there was soil under our feet, Liam stopped.

"Ruar, go for Bhradaín, will you? We need the *scáeli* as witness." The boy didn't seem to mind running the errand, although I wondered for a moment why Liam had not sent him earlier.

"What is it you have to say to me that is not for Ruar's ears?" I asked calmly.

"Only this. I know you to be *channàdarra.* You will not lay a hand on the boy, or you will die."

"I have no interest in boys," I told him, "nor in any man who is uninterested in me. You need not worry, Liam."

He gave a sharp nod, an unpleasant business dealt with. A wind blew off the hills, cold and biting. I wished I had my gloves; chapped fingers fared badly on *ladhar* strings. Ruar returned, with an older man, grey-haired and slightly stooped. Bhradaín, *scáeli* to Dun Ceànnar: if he had been here seven years ago, I would have heard him play. Perhaps even spoken to him. I didn't remember.

"Lord Sorley," Liam said. "As *Raséair* for Ruar, the presumptive *Teannasach* of Linrathe, you will give this oath to me. Do you swear that as a *toscaire* of Linrathe, no man, no prince, no foreign power holds sway over you, and that your loyalty is to the people of Linrathe, and to the land beneath your feet?"

"I so swear," I said. I hoped I spoke the truth.

"Done," Liam said. "Bhradaín, you will record it."

As we returned to the house, Liam told me we would not speak of my instructions as *toscaire* until after Midwinter; until then, I was to think of myself simply as a guest, although if I chose to further

Ruar's education regarding Casil and the Eastern Empire, he would be grateful.

"It would give me great pleasure," I replied, as I had to. During the meal, Liam was as relaxed and pleasant as I had known him. He ate his soup and bread, and then pushed his chair back.

"Stay and talk to Ruar about the East," he said to me. "I have a short sleep after the mid-day meal, when I can. And if you would play for us tonight, we would be honoured. Bhradaín spoke highly of your music. I will see you at dinner."

What did Bhradaín know of my music? Dagney, I supposed. I would have, in the normal course of things, spent part of each year after I left the *Ti'ach* travelling, singing and gathering songs, a requirement for those who aspired to be a *scáeli*. She had likely been writing letters on my behalf. I wondered, idly, what my father would have said: he had expected me to help run the estate. I'd planned on bargaining with him for a few months travelling each year only once I'd arrived home.

But Fritjof had killed his brother and assumed the kingship, and I had never gone home. I never would, now. A sorrow, that. I had spoken to Liam of what I had lost, and I had done it in a way to evoke emotion and compassion. *All those I gave willingly,* I had said. That part was not quite the truth. I had not wanted to give up Sorham, but I had done it because Cillian had told me I should, and Turlo had agreed. I wondered once again if my brother had thought like my father and sided with the Marai. I wondered if he were even alive. I hadn't seen him since he was fifteen.

Not so much older than Ruar. I pulled myself from my reverie. "Is there a map of Linrathe and Sorham?" I asked. "If so, I will show you where we started for the east."

CHAPTER 10

FOR THREE DAYS I was treated exactly as Liam had implied: as the lord Sorley, musician and guest, and nothing more. Other men and a few women arrived: *Eirënnen* and their wives from close *torps*, a few officers from the Sterre. Dun Ceànnar's hospitality at Midwinter was legendary. I played every evening, at Bhradaín's invitation, even tuning my *ladhar* for Casilani melodies, introducing a different music to the audience.

Midwinter's Eve itself, the fire burning high in the huge hearth, I alternated between dancing and conversation, both required of me as lord and *toscaire*, and being a musician. When Bhradaín rested his voice, I played traditional songs, and watched as others danced. Food and ale and *fuisce* were in generous supply, but I wanted a clear head: it would not do for a musician to forget his fingering or the words. I had another reason, too, or a possibility of one. Bhradaín had an apprentice,

Kester, and the boy had been just a little too attentive.

That alone I could have dealt with, but my last conversation with Cillian before I left had been instructive. "*Mo charaidh*, be careful," he had said. "The oath you will swear demands that no man has sway over you. Some—including Liam—may try."

"But on what grounds?"

"You are vulnerable," he said. "Sleep alone, Sorley, even if an overture to you seems freely made." I had said nothing. Cillian had pushed himself a little more upright. "It was not just disgust at my own behaviour that led me to choose a solitary life," he said quietly. "I will tell you, someday. Just be careful."

"I will," I promised. I hadn't needed to be, on the ride north, but this boy worried me. I had noted Kester's occasional covert glance towards Liam after he had helped carry my instrument, or arrange a stool. I had learned to look for certain behaviours, sitting with Cillian over the long days of negotiation in Casil, and I thought it just possible that the boy glanced at Liam to look for approval, not to check if his behaviour towards me had been noticed. I truly hoped the interest was at least in part feigned, or being channelled for his lord's use. Blood would run high tonight, after the music and dancing and the *fuisce*.

Liam shouted for silence, and when the noise died down, offered a toast to the new year.

Bhradaín stepped forward on the low dais, waiting again for silence; then, as befitted his status as *scáeli* to the house, he played and sang the traditional last song of the evening. He was, I thought, listening to the modulation of his voice, very skilled.

Kester appeared at my side. "Can I help you carry your music and instrument to your room, my lord?" he asked softly. He touched my arm.

"Thank you, no," I said, my voice at its usual conversational tone. "I can manage. Help Bhradaín, if he needs it. I wish a word with the *Raséair.*" I stepped off the dais and crossed the floor to where Liam stood, talking to another man.

"*Raséair,*" I said, when he turned to me, with a nod of dismissal to his companion. "Am I to receive my instructions tomorrow?"

"Eager to leave us, are you?" he asked.

"Only that the weather looks to be clear for some days, unless the wind changes." I said, shading my voice towards apology. "At this time of year, a traveller needs to take advantage of that."

"I suppose you are right," he said. "But not too early tomorrow. Late morning. If you wish, you can leave after the mid-day meal, and reach the first *torp* south before nightfall. Thank you for your music tonight. I think Bhradaín's apprentice might prefer to be yours."

"I have no need of an apprentice, or anything else the boy might be induced to offer," I said, quietly but very clearly. I saw the flash of surprise—and annoyance?—in his eyes, quickly masked.

"Good night, Lord Sorley," he said brusquely. "I wish you joy in the new year."

I spoke at length with another guest, one of the Linrathan officers from the Sterre who wanted a first-hand account of the battle along the Wall. We were housed in the same corridor, and we walked together once I had satisfied his curiosity. My room was first, and I turned to it, wishing him goodnight. I opened the door.

Kester sat on the bed, half-undressed, a lamp burning on the table. He looked up, his nearly-black hair falling over his forehead, his eyes dark and huge in the lamplight. Desire shot through me, immediate and demanding.

I stepped back into the corridor. "A minute!" I called to the officer, who turned and came to me. "Look," I said. "I want you to witness that this is how I found him."

"I was invited," Kester said, defiantly.

"He was not," I told the officer, "and Bhradaín will stand as witness to that, I believe. Kester here did indeed offer to bring my instrument to my room, but I refused. The *scáeli* will confirm my words." *Scáeli'en* were sworn to speak the truth, even if unpleasant.

"Put your shirt on, boy, and come with me," my companion barked, frowning. "The *Raséair* will still be awake. Lord Sorley, I suggest you remain here. I will deal with this. If you are needed, I will send someone for you."

I sank onto the bed, still shocked at my reaction. I picked up my *ladhar*, for lack of anything else to do, and let my fingers do what they would. A tune began to emerge, mournful, a lament; a song for night and lamplight, of regret and longing. Words began to form into a verse.

An hour passed. I heard a quiet knock at my door. The Linrathan officer stood there.

"The boy is dealt with," he said. "No blame will be attached to your name, Lord Sorley."

"What will happen to him?" I asked.

He shrugged. "I left that to the *Raséair* and the *scáeli*," he said. "In the army, a flogging, for a first offense. It does little good, if the inclination is there."

"Thank you," I said. "I am sorry I kept you from your bed this night." He wished me goodnight and went off to his room. I closed the door, reached for the *ladhar*, began to sing, softly:

My true love's eyes are softly gleaming
In candlelight and music's lure
One night alone, at spring's fair dawning
To keep me longing through the years
To keep my soul bereft and mourning....

I put the *ladhar* down, weeping. The apprentice had

looked so much like Cillian.

Most of what I discussed with Liam and Ruar the next morning was what I had expected: the considerations for movement across the border; the division of responsibility for troops on the Sterre, locations along the coast where ships of the Empire could take in water or dock for repairs, and a dozen other points. I took notes, explaining that I did not have a memory trained to this. A meeting between Casyn and Liam and Ruar was proposed. Finally, Liam straightened in his chair.

"There is one more thing, Lord Sorley," he said. This would be the most serious, I thought. "There is no action to take on this yet, but the *Princip* and his advisors must be clear on one thing. Linrathe will use whatever means we deem fit to regain Sorham. It is our intent to do so, although it may take many years."

"Noted," I said, keeping my voice neutral.

"And for the tribute we pay to Casil, or will pay, in a year or two, we expect their help."

"Am I to act as your *toscaire* to the Eastern Empire, as well as to the *Princip, Raséair*?" There'd been no mention of this. Negotiate with Decanius? I hadn't the skills.

"For now," he growled. "I will give thought to who might be better suited, but there has been no time. Nor are we planning any attempt to take back Sorham for some years. All you need to do is state our intent. Nothing more. You can do this, I hope?"

"If I must," I said evenly. "Are you thinking of war, *Raséair*?"

"As a last resort," Ruar interjected. "I hope to find peaceful means. My taste of warfare has not whetted my appetite for more, unless there are no other options. I expect I will be fully *Teannasach*, before this plan comes to fruition." I heard a note of rebuke in his voice, directed to his great-uncle.

"If I can be of help, I will be," I said.

"You have promised me that already," Ruar reminded me. "Daylight is short, and you have a distance to ride. You are free to leave, Sorley."

Enough light was left in the day for me to reach a *torp*. I was on the road quickly, riding south.

Dusk and falling snow slowed my pace, but I was on the *Ti'ach's* lands now and I knew this path even in full dark. Approaching from the north, I would come through the small *torp* and past the stables. I would leave my horse there and walk to the *Ti'ach* itself.

As I had reached the first of the cottages, a dog barked. I saw the dull glow of firelight as a door opened and closed. "Who is there?" a voice called.

"Anndra?" I called back. "It's Sorley."

"Sorley!" He stepped forward. I reined my horse to a stop. "The Lady Dagney said you were coming, but why are you at the *torp*, and not the house?"

I dismounted. "I thought I would stable my horse first. I wasn't sure if there would be anyone at the house to take it. How are you, Anndra?"

"Well enough," he said. "Isa too. She'll be up at the house just now. We were that glad to know you were well, after the fighting. And Cillian too. A strange business, with him."

"A long story," I told him. "I wrote a *danta* about it all. Perhaps I will sing it for you, one night before I leave." I had never sung it all, the last verses unfinished in the uncertainty of Cillian's fate. I could devise an ending, now.

"That would be grand," Anndra said. "We'll have a sip or two of *fuisce*, by the fire." He played the *ladhar* himself, with fair skill, and I'd spent more than one evening in his cottage, learning songs.

"No word of Niav?" I asked. His niece, with a singing voice fine enough for her to have been taken on as a student at the *Ti'ach*, Dagney—and I—nurturing and training her.

"None," he said bitterly. "If she's alive, she's been taken north, poor girl. Her, and the Lady Jordis, and many others."

"South of the Wall too," I told him. "And the Lady Dagney, Anndra? How is she?"

"Missing the *Comiádh*," he said, "as you would expect. A sad day, that, when we rang the bell of remembrance for his passing. You will cheer her up. Shall I stable your horse, so you can go to her?"

I slipped in through the kitchen door, putting my saddlebags down on the flagged floor. Isa gave a tiny gasp before she recognized me. "Sorley!" she said. "Frightening me like that!" I grinned at her and gave her a hug.

"I saw Anndra," I told her, as much to prevent her from needing to speak of Niav as anything.

"The Lady Dagney is in her teaching room," she told me. "Go through. I will bring tea in a few minutes. Your room is ready; I've had a fire burning the day, thinking you might come."

I walked across the hall, dark except for a couple of candles on the table. I couldn't quite comprehend that Perras wasn't just behind his study's door. Dagney's door was closed, keeping the warmth in. I knocked and opened it.

She was reading by the fire. Cillian's letter, I thought, glancing at what was in her hands. "Sorley," she said. "How wonderful to see you." She stood, holding out her arms.

There were tears in both our eyes after that embrace. She is older, I thought, watching her composing herself; thinner, more fragile. She must be lonely here.

"I don't know where to start," she said. "You have so much to tell me. Sit. How was Cillian, when you left?"

"He is improving," I told her. "Still in much pain, and not able to be out of bed; there is a long physical recovery ahead of him. The Casilani doctor,

Gnaius—I doubt Cillian would have survived, without his treatments. Gnaius himself would say it was all up to the gods."

"Casil. It is unbelievable. Perras would have so liked to hear your stories."

"Yes," I said sadly. She took my hand.

"He went peacefully," she told me. "Knowing you were both safely home eased him. Even," she said with a rueful smile, "if I bent my *scáeli's* oath in encouraging that belief."

Isa came in with tea, and Dagney and I spoke of my appointment as *toscaire*, and Ruar and Liam, and the travelling I would need to do between the Empire and Linrathe. "Perhaps," she suggested, "you can collect songs, as you travel; we might make a *scáeli* of you yet." She told me of Perras's last weeks, and where he was buried. I would visit the grave in the morning.

"Now, my dear, before we eat, I have a task for you. Would you go to Cillian's room, and choose which books to take back for him?" she asked. "He wants his copy of Catilius, but there may be others as well. And perhaps his clothes?"

"Of course," I said. "I'll do that now." I left her by the fire, and crossed the cold hall to the annex, the added wing of rooms used mostly for guests. I should be housed here, but Isa had given me my old student room, and I had no objections, except that it had meant her aging legs had climbed two flights of stairs to make up the room and tend the fire. I didn't know when Cillian had moved from the boys' floor to his room in the annex: long before I had arrived at the *Ti'ach*. As a journeyman teacher and a *toscaire*, he had certainly been entitled to live separately from the students.

I carried a candle, shielding the flame carefully as I walked. I had never been to Cillian's room; the annex was off-limits to students, even adult ones. Dagney had told me which door. I set the candle on a table against one wall, looking around me. The room was as austere as I might have guessed: a narrow bed with a chest at the foot, a table and chair, the washstand, and a shelf of books. I am trespassing, I thought. But no, Cillian had asked for his book, giving permission for someone to be here.

I found *The Contemplations*, a well-thumbed copy bound in worn leather. It fell open as I took it from the shelf. I glanced down at the text. *In the morning, when you wish to stay asleep, think this*, I read. *I am arising to do a man's work. Is this not my purpose in the world?* I had never heard Cillian quote this line, for all his love of Catilius. I felt slightly embarrassed, as if I had stumbled upon a private note. I closed the book and examined the other titles. There were not many. I would take them all. He might be glad of them in the months of convalescence.

Inside the chest I found a few clothes, neatly folded, and below them, a drawstring bag. I took it out, reluctant to open it. The contents shifted in my hand, and I realized what must be inside. I loosened the drawstring, letting the *xache* pieces spill out onto the bed. They were carved of wood, and small, made for a child's hands. The wood had the patina of long use. Perhaps made for him by his grandfather; perhaps older than that. He would want these, in a few years, for his own son or daughter. But by then, I thought, he and Lena and the child should be here. And I? It was what he wanted. What I wanted. I would leave the game in the chest.

After a simple supper, we retired again to Dagney's teaching rooms. It did not surprise me when she turned the conversation again to Cillian. "Do you know what is in this letter?" she asked.

"No," I answered.

"A request," she said, "that I come to Wall's End, as a *scáeli* of Linrathe, to marry him and Lena. Now tell me, Sorley: is this only to make his child legitimate in this country?"

"What has he said?" I asked, frowning.

"Just that he and Lena had paired, during their exile, and that the child is due at the end of winter, and he wishes it to be legitimate."

I smiled at Dagney, wryly. "He is heavily drugged, and perhaps that was all he could manage, or trust himself to say. Dagney, Cillian loves Lena with all his heart. He is a changed man in many ways, and has been since we met them in the wilds. It is not all her doing; there is a story there, but it should be Cillian's to tell you. But to hear his voice when he calls her *käresta* is a story—no, a song—in itself."

"I am so glad," she said softly. "And she returns his love?"

"Completely."

"You can accept this, my dear? Your own letter was quite brief, too."

"I apologize for that," I said. "It was written at a difficult time. I long ago accepted that he loves Lena. Cillian and I are friends now in a way I would have never thought possible, almost brothers." I had never openly revealed my nature to Dagney, but it was clear she knew. "And I have a companion now, a soldier from Casil who returned with us. He's a musician, too. Druisius, his name is, and in the Empire, we can be together openly. "

"Another joy, then," she murmured.

"Yes." I hesitated. I would need her approval of an idea that I had had, on the ride south, if she were the *scáeli* performing the marriage. "When I turned sixteen," I said, "my father gave me a set of *li'ítho* bracelets, as is the custom. I do not know if he was genuinely blind, or simply hoping that I would give in and marry, to at least father an heir. I will never use them, of course. I was thinking—perhaps—to give them to Cillian and Lena."

She considered. "Cillian will say he is not entitled to them, as they are a custom of the nobility," she pointed out.

"And would not the son of the Emperor be considered noble, by our standards?" I countered.

"True," she said. "But are you sure?" I understood her unspoken question.

"A gift," I said. "Offered in friendship for them both. Nothing more. Should they lie unused in a chest?"

"I suppose not," she said eventually. "If Cillian and Lena will accept the *li'ítho*, I can perform the ceremony that includes them. It is a generous offer, my dear."

"The child is due in under three months," I said. "When will you come?"

"If you will act as my escort, I will ride south to Wall's End with you, in a day or so. Would I be welcome to stay a while, do you think?"

"I imagine the *Princip* will be honoured," I told her. "Your presence can only speed Cillian's recovery."

Walking up the stairs to my old room felt strange. I had been a boy—for all my twenty-three years— when I left. No longer. A peat fire scented the room, glowing red, and the small space was warm enough. My bags sat neatly against the wall. But otherwise the room was as bare as Cillian's had been.

That stark space had disturbed me. When I had lived in this room, I had made it mine, as much as possible. A blanket woven at our *torp* and dyed in our family's colours had covered the bed; a wood

142

carving of a sheepdog, from the hands of one of our *torpari*, sat on the shelves, beside a seal-shaped pebble I had picked up along the strand as a child and kept ever since. My music had littered the table, and often the floor. Cillian had left his room for a short journey north with Donnalch, expecting to return to it in a few weeks, so he had not prepared it to sit empty for a long time. It was simply the way he had lived, and the barrenness of it made me want to weep.

Was my reaction only to the contrast between the detached and unhappy man he had been, and the loving, generous friend he had become? All those years he spent alone looking for meaning in an ancient, ascetic philosophy. I had read Catilius, and while I'd found some good advice in his writing, I'd also found a lot I couldn't accept. Catilius had not approved of love between men, and made that clear, but that was only part of it. He'd disapproved of any pleasure, it seemed to me, and had said nothing at all about music. Life was for work, and personal discipline.

Cillian's room had reflected that: a place to sleep, alone; to read and write, perhaps, and nothing more. But why did that unsettle me? I frowned, trying to analyse my feelings. I looked at Cillian's books, stacked on the table. Catilius had guided his life for twenty years or more: how easily could he let those teachings go, truly? Especially with the book to hand, and the adjustments to pain and disability and loss he had to make. I do not envy you, Lena, I thought.

All the confusion I had felt for the last weeks rose again. *I love you,* Lena had told him in my hearing at Casil, *as difficult and complicated and flawed as you are. And I*, I had added. It had been true, and it was still true. I loved Cillian, but I didn't want a difficult and complicated life. I wanted simple and uncomplicated. I wanted music and a wide bed and a man who was teaching me about who I was. I wanted Druise.

CHAPTER 11

WE LEFT TWO DAYS LATER, Dagney on her placid mare and a packhorse carrying baggage being led behind. I had sung the *danta* of our exploits in the east the night before, for the *torpari* and Dagney, in the hall of the *Ti'ach*. They were my first audience, apart from those of us on the ship home.

"Another accomplishment to be put against your name," Dagney had told me afterwards. "Sorley, shall I inform the council that you wish to be examined? Your travel to Casil, and gathering songs from there, and this *danta*, are almost enough now. If you could add songs from the Empire to your repertoire as well, I believe that would tip the balance. If this is something you still want?"

Could I truly be a *scáeli*? Not while I was a *toscaire*: the *scáeli's* requirement to tell the truth conflicted with the necessary deceptions of an envoy. But the title could be conferred in principle, to be granted in full when I was no longer a *toscaire*. "Something I want?" I said, wonder and a disbelieving hope spreading through me. "Dagney, do you have to ask? I hadn't thought it possible."

"There will have to be some change to the requirements," she said, "if travel in Sorham and Varsland are no longer possible. One of many changes, I suppose, that will occur over the next years."

When we reached the Wall and a guard post the next day, I had a messenger sent ahead, to alert Wall's End to Dagney's arrival. Riding at speed, he would reach the fort several hours before us.

The western sky glowed in shades of pink and gold as we rode into the fort. Cadets came to take horses and baggage, and I led Dagney into the low infirmary building. She wanted, she had told me, to see Cillian first, before anything else. And, she added, she would take on the sad task of telling him of Perras's death. It was her responsibility.

I hoped he would be awake, and not too heavily drugged. The door was slightly ajar, which I took as a good sign. I knocked, with the triple rap I used to tell him it was me, and gestured Dagney into the room.

"Oh, my dear man," she said. Over her shoulder I could see Cillian sitting—sitting!—in a chair, his left leg on a footstool. Lena sat close to him; they had been talking, I thought.

"Dagney!" he said, smiling slowly, "I am afraid you must come to me. I do apologize."

She crossed the room to him. I caught Lena's eye, smiled, and with a movement of my head indicated I would leave. She held up a hand to ask me to wait.

"I will leave you," she said. "I am so glad you are here, Dagney. I'll come back in a while, and show you to your room, and the baths if you would like. If you are not too tired, the *Princip* will be honoured if you will join him at dinner."

"You do not need to go, Lena," Dagney protested.

"I'll come back," Lena said, "but you should have some private time together right now." She bent to kiss Cillian. "Do not tire yourself," she told him.

"I will try not to. Sorley, *mo charaidh*, come and greet me properly," he called. I went to crouch beside his chair for an embrace and the brief kiss of welcome.

"You are so much better," I murmured.

"A long way to go," he said, "but better, yes." He sounded uncertain, his voice hesitant.

I straightened. "A half hour, *käresta*," Cillian said to Lena. I glanced at Dagney, seeing both worry and wonder on her face. Worry for his health; wonder at hearing him call Lena *beloved*. She had not, I thought, quite believed me.

"We will bring tea," Lena said.

"Welcome back," she said in the corridor, giving me a hug. Her belly was larger, with only a bit over two months to go. She leaned against me, as if needing the support.

"How is he, really?" I asked.

"Not good," she said bluntly. "He is putting on a brave face for Dagney."

"But he says he is better."

"With help, and the two walking sticks, he can get up and move a few steps, but the left leg drags. Tears rose in her eyes. "Oh, Sorley. He is in so much pain, and dependent on Druise for almost everything. He hates that. Cillian never wanted to ask anyone for anything, and now he is little better than an infant again. And he hates the poppy juice, as you can imagine."

"It will improve," I said, rubbing her back.

"Maybe. Gnaius will only say maybe." She began to cry in earnest. I pulled her closer, letting her lean against my shoulder.

"Tell me."

"He may never walk properly. He may never make love again. And his mind...Gnaius does not know if the dullness and confusion is the poppy and other drugs, or damage. Cillian knows he cannot think properly, and he is angry and frightened."

"And Cillian angry and frightened is Cillian cold and sarcastic?" I asked, as gently as I could.

She shook her head. "No. But detached, distant. I am so afraid for him. Sorley—please stay with us? Cillian needs you, for his own language, and music, and something more."

What did it cost her, to ask me this? I had suggested in Casil that she and I needed each other, to cope with Cillian's brilliance. And his darkness, she had added later. This was a responsibility older than my relationship with Druise. "For as long as you need me, Lena," I told her.

"Thank you," she whispered. "You are my anchor right now. If you left us…" She ran out of words.

"I'm not going to," I told her firmly. "Not more than my *toscaire's* duties require. Absences, not abandonment."

She straightened, wiping her eyes. "Should you not go to find Druise? I can fetch tea. Bring Druise back, if you wish, to share it with us. Unless," she said, sudden concern on her face, "Dagney?"

"I told Dagney about him," I said. "She knows what I am. "

Lena frowned. "What you are?" she said. "Sorley, do you not hear yourself? You are a musician and, right now, an envoy. That is what you are. That you share your bed with men is as natural to you as your blue eyes. Why do you judge yourself on it?"

I felt heat rise in my face. "Why do you think?"

"Linrathe and Sorham are wrong, not you," she said. And yet, I thought, Cillian wanted to return to Linrathe, and he wanted me to go with him. Without Druise, and without the freedom to be myself I had found here. Even at the open-minded *Ti'ach.*

That reminded me. "Lena," I said, "Dagney will be

telling Cillian of Perras's death. How will he be?"

"Bereft," she said. "We have been talking, these past days, of how Dagney and Perras were almost foster-parents to him. He has been thinking about being a father; it frightens him, you know."

"Then perhaps Druise and I should not join you for tea? Will he not want just you?"

"You can speak to him of Perras. I can, a little, of course, but not in the same way. Join us. You will know if he wants you there, but, Sorley, since Casil, when has he ever not? He has missed you, these weeks."

Cillian looked tired, and saddened, but he made an effort again in our presence. I introduced Druise to Dagney. She charmed him with a few words in Casilan; he was growing better with the language of the Empire, so as a group, we could converse without too many translations needed.

We'd been talking for ten minutes or so when Druise's attention turned to Cillian. "You need poppy," he said firmly.

"No," Cillian said. "Not yet."

"Yes," Druisius said. He switched to Casilan. "You are over an hour past your time," he said, "and you have been up far too long. Poppy, and bed. Do not argue."

I don't know if Dagney understood the Casilan, or just the tone of Druisius's voice. "I am tired," she said. "Lena, did you mention baths? That would be most welcome. And is there time for a rest, before dinner?" She stood. "Cillian, my dear, I will see you tomorrow." She held out a hand to him. He took it, raising it to his lips.

"I know when I am bested," he said. "The baths for you, then, and poppy and bed for me. I am glad you are here, Dagney."

He dropped the pretence once the women had left. Pain tightened his neck and jaw. "I will need help to stand," he said. I stepped forward, but Druise shook his head. Expertly he held out both arms, letting Cillian grasp them, then pulling him up and, at the same time, towards him, so that Cillian stood straight but supported. Druise waited until Cillian nodded before reaching for the crutches.

"You have them?" he asked, and at Cillian's assent let go of his arms,

It was no more than half a dozen steps to the bed, but watching Cillian walk that distance tore at my heart. His left leg would not bear his weight, and his lower body twisted with each step. He lowered himself to the bed, and Druisius lifted his legs up and slid him towards the centre. "Deep breaths."

Once Cillian was on the bed, Druise mixed poppy syrup with wine and a little water. "Drink," he ordered. "Maybe Sorley will play for you."

"Sorley," Cillian said, haltingly. "*Allech'i*... for Perras..."

Tears glittered in his eyes. Not from the physical pain, I thought, and felt the answering sting in my own. "*Thá*," I murmured, and, taking the *ladhar* down from where it hung on the wall, I played the ancient lament, the parting song.

Druise stopped what he was doing, listening. The pipes would be played at a grave, but we were not there, and they were not my instrument. I played the last three notes slowly, letting each resonate and fade before the next: one note for forgiveness, one for loss, and one for love.

I put the *ladhar* down and with fingers as gentle as I could make them, I wiped the tears from Cillian's cheeks. "*Meas*," he whispered. I kissed his forehead, not caring if Druise saw. Then I picked up my instrument again and played lullabies until Cillian's breathing told me he was asleep. Simple and uncomplicated had been a fleeting wish, nothing more, as naïve as the cradle songs I had been playing.

Druise lay on the bed, watching me dress. I had brought my formal clothes from the *Ti'ach*, the breeches and tunic grey, trimmed with green, and the cloak of green-and-grey plaid, the colours of Gundarstorp. "Will you be late?"

"I shouldn't think so. Dagney must be tired. I am not the *toscaire*, tonight, or I don't think I am."

"The *Princip* comes to talk to Cillian now, sometimes. Late mornings, when the poppy has worked but he is not yet asleep."

"About what?"

"The Marai. Casil. He seeks advice, on both."

"Should he be bothering Cillian with this?"

"Why not? It is good for him." He stretched. "I will do his exercises, when you go to dinner."

I remembered something. I went to my bags. "Take this to him, will you?" I asked, holding out Catilius. "He asked for it."

Druise opened it, reading a few words. "I have heard of this book," he said, "Not just from Cillian, I mean, but from before."

"Druise? Does it bother you, that you are left out of these dinners?" It had been nagging at me.

"No," he said, surprised.

"Lena will be there," I pointed out.

"Lena is an officer, and Cillian's *quincala*, and soon his wife, yes? And she has known the *Princip* for many years. I am happy to eat with the soldiers, Sorley. Do not worry."

Dagney was tired, and so while dinner was a formal welcome for her, it was also not a long evening. But after Dagney rose to leave, Lena with her, Casyn spoke to me. "A minute, Lord Sorley?"

"*Princip*?"

He signalled to Birel to pour more wine before dismissing him. Official business, then. I waited. "I will not keep you," he said. "One question only: what did you think of Liam?"

"He can be trusted, *Princip*," I answered. "My judgement, based on both what I learned riding north and my observations there, tell me that." He nodded. "Perhaps there is one message from them I should give you now," I said. "For your consideration, before we address all the other issues which my instructions require me to discuss with you, over the next weeks."

"Certainly, then."

I told him what Liam had vowed: that Linrathe would regain Sorham, by any means necessary. "There will be no immediate action. This is an avowal, not a call to arms. But the *Raséair* expects Casil's assistance, for the tribute paid in future years."

"The regent? Not the young *Teannasach*?"

"At this moment, Ruar considers diplomatic means preferable."

"I am glad to hear that. But who has the real power, Sorley?"

"The *Eirënnen* and the *torpari* speak of Ruar as the *Teannasach*, regardless of his age. He took his sword into battle to defend Linrathe against the Marai, and in their eyes that makes him their leader. Or at least that is how the more southern landholders regard him. In the *torps* around Dun Ceànnar and the Sterre, where Liam is a powerful figure, the opinion may be different. I could not determine that."

"I see." He drank a little wine. "I seek Cillian's opinion sometimes, on various matters, but he is reluctant to give it. He does not trust his memory, or his reasoning, he says; the drugs cloud his mind."

"Have you asked him about Liam?" I asked, recalling our conversation before I had ridden north. "He expressed clear opinions to me."

"I did, yes," Casyn said. "And I agree: he was very certain. A subtle mind, he said, and devious, but with Linrathe's welfare his first consideration. A reluctant admiration, I thought."

"And I must take direction from Liam," I said. "Although direction only; my decisions are my own, as to what is best for my country and my people."

"You can disobey him?"

"Yes. My oath is to the land, and I have sworn that no man holds sway over me. That includes the *Teannasach*, and his regent. In practice *toscairen* are neutral, gathering information, reporting it, delivering responses, but if I believed a decision was contrary to what was best for Linrathe, I could decline to give the message, or counsel against it. I can refuse any task for the same reason, without reprisal."

"Colm told me once that the custom in your land is that all men are equal; that a shepherd considers himself no different from the *Teannasach* in terms of his worth."

"He spoke correctly. One of Ruar's uncles—Liam's daughters' husbands—is an *Eirën's* son, but the other was a bright *torpari* boy, sent to the *Ti'ach na Asgaill* to be educated. Men are judged by their skills and their minds, not by their father's position."

"As long as there is a father."

"Cillian was—is—respected, for his intelligence and insight," I said. "But Linrathe's people, and Sorham's, claim kinship and—" I searched for a translation, but I did not know the word for *dùthcas* in Casyn's language, "belonging, through their fathers. Cillian had no family, and no place to call home."

"For men of the Empire," Casyn said, "home is their regiment, wherever it is sent. A boy is claimed by his father, or his father's regiment. Perhaps it is not so different."

"You see commonalities," I observed, "where others see contrasts."

"Do I? I tend to think men have the same wants and needs, wherever we are from. Perhaps even Decanius," he added with a wry grin. Over the months, I had come to like the *Princip* very much. Endlessly patient in the negotiations, but capable of firmly expressing his disapproval, his sardonic remarks in private revealed an amused understanding of men. I wondered what he said about me.

"Possibly," I said. Casyn laughed.

"You must be tired. Have you things to address with me, now you are officially Linrathe's *toscaire*?"

"Nothing difficult," I told him. "Details of troops on the Sterre, and the like."

"Turlo can deal with that. Begin with him, if you

will: he is eager to return north, and I would prefer not to delay him more than necessary. Turlo," he added, "does not like forts."

"Or palaces," I said. "He escaped to the docks in Casil whenever he could."

"We have asked much of him, Callan and I," the *Princip* said. "But who among us can do only what we prefer, in these times? Or any, I suppose."

Turlo might be eager to escape the confines of Wall's End, but he did not stint on discussing the details of patrolling the Sterre. Maps and game pieces, like the ones Callan had used to show the positions of Marai and the Empire's forces in his workroom at the Eastern Fort littered the table, and by the time we were done, I knew more about the landscape on either side of the Sterre than I had ever thought I would. "I worry about the eastern end," he told me, "where the earthworks meet the Durrains. I want more men there. Galen tells me it is not too difficult to move across the slopes above it, well out of sight."

"Linrathe never looked east for its enemies," I said. "Only north."

"Aye, and south, once," Turlo reminded me. "It is strange to see the Wall undefended, except for cohorts at the watchtowers."

"Another thing I must discuss," I said, "the conditions for movement across the border."

"That is for Casyn, not me," Turlo said.

"I suppose it is," I said, "as it is open and permitted travel we will be discussing, and not covert reconnaissance." Turlo had told me quite a few stories on our journey east. He barked with laughter.

"Aye, laddie. But knowing secret ways is useful. Are we done?"

I looked at my notes. "I think so. I will need to send the details to Dun Ceànnar for approval."

"Get it written, and I'll take the report north. Easier now for me to argue the fine points with the Linrathan commander than to go back and forth with messengers and letters," he suggested.

"Not to mention you can leave sooner," I said. He didn't disagree.

CHAPTER 12

I TOOK MY PAPERS to the room that I had taken over as my study. I needed to clear my mind before attempting the report, and I hadn't seen Cillian since the previous day. Druise had said he'd be at his best in the late morning.

He was out of bed, talking with Casyn. "Shall I come back?" I asked.

"We were talking of the Marai, of the kinship and allegiances among them," Casyn said. "There are links to Sorham, too, are there not?"

"Many," I said, pulling up a seat. "Both through marriages and through trade arrangements. The Marai traded for wool from Gundarstorp and our neighbours, and sometimes for fish as well."

"What did they offer in return?"

"Hides, ivory, sometimes metalwork. And horses."

"Horses?" Casyn asked.

"Ponies, really, but large and strong. Solid. We

used them for riding and draught work at Gundarstorp; better than our own hill ponies, and with a good temperament."

"I remember your horse," Cillian said. "Grey, wasn't it?"

"Grey dun, yes," I said, oddly pleased.

"And your brother's was paler."

"They are all shades of dun," I said, surprised he remembered what I had ridden at Gundarstorp, "from nearly white to almost black."

"Fritjof's son rode a white horse at the Taiva," Casyn said, "to fool our troops into thinking he was Callan. Our own symbol, used against us." I remembered Turlo's unabashed tears when he saw the flag of the Empire, the white horse and the Wall, still flying as we sailed into sight of the Eastern Fort, returning from Casil.

"Has the Procurator insisted that Casil's flag be flown?" Cillian asked. His thoughts had reflected mine, I guessed. Making connections.

"Yes," Casyn said heavily. "He has allowed ours to be flown beneath it, until, he says, the troops have learned to identify the eagle as their flag. As if an order to do so is not sufficient."

"He is used to illiterate troops," Cillian said, "and has not bothered to discover that ours are not."

Casyn's eyes narrowed. "And he will not, I wager, exert himself to learn to read our language."

"A way to communicate with our troops, then, openly but secretly?" Cillian said softly. My eyes went from one to the other, these two men discussing how they might deceive their Empress's representative.

"Be very careful," I heard myself say. "Randall speaks and writes both languages."

"You do not trust him?" Casyn asked sharply.

"I think," I said, trying to give substance to instinct, "that he may be easily swayed. We were speaking just the other day, *Princip*, about the worth of men in Linrathe, do you remember? Randall is an exception, it seems to me: he should consider us as equals, as we both spent five years at a *Ti'ach*, but he cannot forget I am Lord Sorley. Decanius is the type who will recognize that in him, and use it."

"Liam's factor's son? He attended the *Ti'ach na Asgaill*?" Cillian asked.

"Yes," I replied. "He was sent here to teach Casilan to our officers, but he has been acting as Decanius's translator, as I could not."

"I taught him, for a winter. Casilan, as it happens. That tendency to resentment was there, certainly, but he was young. You say it has not changed? Then I would concur with Sorley, Casyn: be careful of him."

"Thank you, both of you" Casyn said. "Cillian, do you see that your advice is worth having?"

"On certain things, perhaps," Cillian answered. "Not strategy. Not yet."

When Casyn left, I smiled at Cillian. "You are

sounding more like yourself."

"My thoughts are a little clearer. I wonder…" His voice trailed off.

"What?"

"Could you come tomorrow at this time, when I am at my best, and we will attempt a game of *xache*?"

"Certainly." I grinned. "Is it unfair of me to say I look forward to the chance of beating you?" I was rewarded by the flash of a smile.

"Taking pleasure in besting an ill man?"

"Ill you may be, Cillian, but you will still win at *xache*," I told him.

I was wrong, and it was clear after the opening moves. I didn't speak while Cillian studied the game, reaching for a piece, then withdrawing, unsure. His eyes moved over the board. Finally he pushed a piece forward, then immediately shook his head.

I pretended to consider, although my move was obvious. "Don't," he said. "You know what to play: do it." I took his piece. He exhaled, his lips thinning.

"I can't see the pattern," he said. "I know what the pieces do, but I can't hold it in my head."

"It's too soon," I suggested. "Perhaps we should wait a week or two more."

"Or perhaps I will never see the pattern again," he said flatly.

"You cannot know that. Not while you need the

poppy."

"How long will that be? All my life?"

"Surely not," I protested.

"It is possible," he said. "What use am I, Sorley, if I cannot think; cannot see patterns in men's thoughts and behaviour?"

"Do you have to be of use, Cillian? Cannot you just let yourself recover? And this," I indicated the *xache* board, "is just a game."

"Is it? Consider how you would feel, if your fingers forgot what to do on your *ladhar's* strings."

Lost and bereft, I admitted to myself. I would not know who I was. "I could not play for some time after the battles," I said, stretching the truth. "I took a swordcut to my arm. I gave it time to heal cleanly. *Mo duíne gràhadh*, put the board aside, with the pieces in place. Study it at your leisure. We will play slowly. Did you not tell me once of two scholars who took years over a game, exchanging moves by letter?"

"Perras told you, not I," he answered. He looked at the board again. "I suppose we can try. Perhaps in solitude I will see what I cannot now. Leave me, *mo charaidh.* I am not fit company."

"Do you want one of your books, before I go?"

"Yes. There is one there by Serventius: Gnaius gave it to me. A translation from the Heræcrian. He influenced Catilius greatly, but I knew of him only by name." I found the small, bound book, handing it to him. He had sounded happier again, speaking of the writing. An idea budded. I bent to kiss his head.

"Don't brood," I said. He didn't smile. I left him, and went to find Gnaius.

"I do not know," the physician said in answer to my first question. "Long fever, and high, can damage the faculties of thought. But poppy clouds and confuses also. Until we can wean him of the drug, we will not have an answer."

"When will that be?"

"Not until he can walk properly, or nearly so. He needs the drug to mask the pain: if he does not have it, his body will contort, finding ways to move that hurt less, do you see? That will become first habit and then fixed, and he will never be anything but crippled, reliant always on two sticks and moving only a few steps. I believe we can better that, but not without poppy."

I would not wish Cillian a crippled body any more than I would a crippled mind. He had been grace itself when I had first met him. I remembered him dancing at Gundarstorp, to the music I'd been playing.

Forcing my mind back to what I had come for, I asked my second question.

"Of course," Gnaius said, sounding just the tiniest bit affronted. "I was a student at the finest school in Casil."

"Then..." I explained my idea. He raised an elegant eyebrow.

"I could," he said. "It might be instructive. An experiment. Will Cillian agree?"

"Almost certainly."

"Then we will begin tomorrow."

The days of cold and snow just before midwinter had given way to a mild spell; mild and dry, an unusual combination. No one objected; less fuel was needed for the fort and barracks, and neither horses nor men broke legs on ice, or became mired in mud. Druisius complained, good-naturedly, and wore the cloak and gloves I had given him, even on days when I went outside only in my tunic and breeches.

Turlo returned north, his tolerance for the restrictions of the fort at its end. "It is not just the fort," Casyn told me one day, after we had concluded our business. "We are too close to Berge, and he cannot forget what happened there. What we let happen to the woman he loved, and to others. He is better on the Sterre."

We had been talking of movement across the border, allowing people from Linrathe to come south, to find employment in the villages or Casilla. "Tell the *Teannasach* not yet," Casyn had said. "This survey of our lands and the census of our people that the Procurator has begun must be completed first. He said a year, before he returned to the

Eastern Fort; less if Casil sent more men to work on it in the spring."

"But it will be allowed then?"

"Can I say?" He had sounded tired. "Sorley, increasingly I think *Princip* is a meaningless title, and I will be allowed to make nothing but decisions that do not matter. What is Decanius's phrase—'A modern province of Casil'? What do I know about that?"

"You know your people, *Princip*," I said. "How they will see these changes."

"Perhaps. But if I have no power to gainsay what Decanius imposes, what good is knowing my people? But this is not your concern. What else do we need to decide?"

"Just a list of places deemed appropriate for the ships that patrol the coast to stop to take in water, or make repairs. Harbours deep enough, or sheltered enough."

"I do not need to see it," he said. "I will ask the commander of the northern fleet to meet with you."

"As you wish, *Princip*."

"Is that all?" I had told him yes, and he'd leaned back in his chair. "I miss Turlo, and his advice, but I could not ask him to stay. I had hoped Cillian would be more willing to counsel me. But he refuses, still."

"He doubts himself," I said.

"Does he blame himself for what happened at the Taiva?" Casyn asked. "I cannot bring myself to ask him."

"If he does, he hasn't told me. But were I to guess, knowing Cillian, yes."

"Callan would have taken the blame, too, had he lived," the *Princip* said. "They are very alike, Sorley, in so many ways, and yet Cillian is like Colm too. The best of both twins, in one man."

"The best man I have ever known."

"He engenders an unusual depth of loyalty, that is certain. Birel tells me that Druisius says he is the finest officer he has served, and that I do find—interesting. Coming as it does from your *consor*."

"Druise," I said, "is a pragmatic man. We are good companions, with the music in common, and our partnership suits us both."

"Regardless of your complex loyalties," Casyn said. "A friend worth having."

"Sorley, will you stay, so if I am not back when Cillian returns from his treatments, you are here?" Lena asked late one morning. "He will be in pain, until the poppy begins to work, and you will distract him."

"Of course," I answered. "But where are you going?"

"For a walk. I need to be outside for a while. You don't mind?"

"Don't be foolish," I said. I settled down with my *ladhar*, working on the song I had promised Casyn.

I wasn't getting anywhere with it: I simply hadn't known Callan well enough, and I wanted it to be more than a standard tribute. I could write a tune, but would it fit the words?

Perhaps an hour had passed when I heard a knock at the door. "I was looking for Lena," Talyn said to my greeting.

"She's gone for a walk," I told her. "But that was some time ago; I expect her back soon. Come in." I didn't know Talyn well; she'd come a few times, when Cillian was still unconscious, but we'd never exchanged more than a word or two. "Cillian and Druisius are with Gnaius. I'd be glad of the company."

She gave a little shrug. "If you think Lena won't mind."

"Of course not. Wine?"

"Yes. Why not?" She sat down. I handed her the cup, placed the water jug on the table, and sat across from her. "So," she said. "Lord Sorley. How were the horses I gave you, long months ago?"

"The horses?" I asked. I'd been sent to her for mounts to take Ruar and myself and our guide north along the Durrains from the Eastern Fort, a hard ride to reach and rally the men of Linrathe against the Marai there, to keep them from marching south to the Taiva. "I'm still riding the gelding. Did you want him back?"

She laughed. "No. Consider him yours. I wanted to know if the cohort-seconds chose well, that's all."

"They did. Should Linrathe pay for the others? I left them at Ruar's camp."

She shook her head. "Your countrymen are welcome to them. A small thank you, shall we say?"

"I will let Ruar know." I groped for something to say. "You have bred horses all your life?"

"Yes. It's what we do, in the grasslands, horses and cattle, both mostly for the army. Oh, some of us are blacksmiths, or harness-makers, and of course we have midwives and woodworkers and tanners, but the midwife can deliver a baby or a foal, and we all ride. It's what brought my father there originally: at Festival in our villages, the men come for the usual reasons, but also to take the horses we have broken and trained for them away. Casyn was sent as a blacksmith, to help ours shoe the animals for travel. My mother said she fell in love with him when she saw how gentle he was with the horses."

"You know him well? I didn't think that was usual, here."

"It isn't. But he came back, every year, and frequently for both Festivals, even after my mother died. They loved each other, and he loved us, me and my sister. We looked forward to seeing him as children, and as we grew into adulthood, we had the horses and their training in common." She smiled. "I remember my mother's partner Jesa swearing he was trying to make soldiers of us, when he showed us what men needed the horses to be able to do in battle. How little she knew how prophetic her words would be."

"Your mother's partner?" I said. "But did you not just say—"

"That she loved my father? She did. But two weeks a year, and not always that, if he was posted too far away? Would you live that way, Lord Sorley? She loved her partner too, and Jesa her. But when Festival came, Jesa took herself off to sleep in the stables—and not alone, I am sure—and left their big bed to my parents."

"I see," I said. "Forgive me, Talyn. I am still learning. North of the Wall, life is different. Although men—especially those who are noble— do bed women other than their wives. And if I am truthful, those wives who have produced the requisite heirs have their own freedoms." Many a noble wife in Sorham worked every day with women her husband bedded, and the welcome given by *Konë* and *Härra* to certain *scáeli'en* and *toscairen* was known, if rarely openly acknowledged, by their husbands. A different way to spread ideas, and to learn what women thought but might not say in front of their men.

I tore my thoughts away from that path. "Not so

different, then," Talyn said, "except that here our freedoms are for everyone, and for all pairings. Which I understand is not true in your land?"

"No. What I am—my nature—is shunned there. Worse than shunned."

"But there are always men who want only men, just as there are women who want only women. What do you do?"

"Live that part of our lives in shadows," I said, hearing the bitterness in my voice. "Shadows and corners, and in fear."

"How terrible." She sounded as if she meant it. "Everywhere?"

"It is a little better, among the *scáeli'en*, and around those who are educated at a *Ti'ach*, like Cillian," I admitted. "But all must be secret, still. Not like Casil, or here."

"You were Cillian's lover, then?"

"Gods, no," I said. "No. He is not—he is my friend, nothing more."

"I have misunderstood, then," she said. "I thought Lena had told me differently. My apologies, Lord Sorley."

"What Lena will have told you is that I love him," I said bluntly. "I do. It is not returned, not in that way. It is not his nature."

"And if it were?"

Puzzlement wrinkled my brow. "He is vowed to

Lena. They will marry soon."

"But this is not Linrathe, or Sorham. Freedoms are for everyone, and we do not understand the limitations of marriage."

"Cillian does," I said.

"Lena's ideas may be different," she countered. Then she leaned back, spreading her hands. "And now I must apologize again. I am offending you, without meaning to, aren't I? When I was only trying to show you that you may see things here that are different, but that to us are normal." She grinned. "I should leave diplomacy to my cousin, I think. Shall we talk of something else? Tell me about what a...a *scáeli,* is that the word? does."

I would be churlish if I did not accept the apology. "I wasn't offended," I assured her, "just surprised. These ideas, as I said, are new to me. A *scáeli,* Talyn, is a travelling musician, but much more than that. He or she is a historian, the holders and disseminators of our deeds and stories, in the form of songs." We spoke of music and the teaching of history for some minutes, until Talyn put down her empty wine cup.

"Lena must have gone for a long walk," she said. "The sun is shining, and it isn't cold, so I'd guess she's just enjoying the day. I had best return to my work. Thank you for the wine and conversation, Lord Sorley."

"No title," I said. "Please."

At the door she stopped, turning to look at me. "Only men for you, Sorley?"

I smiled, involuntarily. "Only men, Talyn."

"Pity," she said, returning the smile. "I like you. Tell Lena I was here, will you?"

"I will," I said. When Talyn had gone, I didn't feel like going back to the song. I'd have to get the *Princip* to tell me stories about his brother, I decided. Where was Lena? I walked over to the window, opening the shutters wider to look out. Behind me, the door opened.

I didn't need Lena to speak to tell me she was angry. Every muscle radiated tension. "What's wrong?"

"Berge," she said, her jaw tight. "I went to Berge, a women's village, Sorley. No one wanted to talk to me; they were barely polite."

"Gods, Lena, why? They should be thanking you, for killing Fritjof."

She stalked over to the sideboard to pour herself wine. Without asking she handed me a cup too. "Maybe they should. But what they see is a woman who wasn't brutalized by the Marai, and who carries a child conceived in love. Or so Kyreth told me, when she asked me to leave."

"Kyreth?" She was the midwife, and she came to see Lena weekly. "She thinks that too?"

"No." Lena sighed, sinking into a chair. "She says her concerns are the babies, and the health of the mothers, but that my presence upsets too many pregnant girls—and they are girls, many of them, Sorley—and so I should not come again."

I started to rub her shoulders. She leaned back into my hands. "Maybe after the baby is born?" I suggested."

"No. She is the problem, really, I think. The Marai did not reach the grassland villages, or Casilla, so those women escaped capture and rape as well. But a child born of love reminds the women of Berge of what they have lost. Even my own sister expressed doubt she could love the child she carried, when I saw her in Casilla, months ago."

I had no advice to offer; how could I? I bent to kiss her on the temple. "You have us," I said. "And the *Ti'ach*, someday."

"I know. I'd already realized I couldn't go back to Tirvan, but I wanted it to be my choice. And that isn't why I'm angry. How dare they judge my child on how she was fathered?"

"Because theirs will be," I said gently.

She exhaled, loudly. Her hands were still clenched. "But why should they be? I told Cillian once that if...if Ivor had left me pregnant, I didn't think I could have loved the child. He reminded me it would have been innocent, and he was right." She reached for her wine, draining the cup. "I will not expose our child to hatred, Sorley. I will marry Cillian, and go home with him to the *Ti'ach*. The sooner the better."

CHAPTER 13

WINE WITH THE *PRINCIP* became part of my day more and more frequently, Casyn sending Birel to find me even on days when we had had no business together. "Who else is there?" Lena said, when I commented on it to her. "His brothers are dead; Turlo is on the Sterre. Bren?"

"Leste," I said, "I believe. Or maybe the Eastern Fort."

"Casyn was always a man for reflection," she said. "At Tirvan, he ended most days with Dern—he was captain of *Skua*, the ship sent to support us—over food and wine. Or with Gille, once they had paired for those few weeks."

"He should be talking to Cillian."

"He tries. Cillian will not talk of the negotiations; only of philosophy and history." She sighed. "He spends more time with his books, paying less attention to what is happening around him, every day. How can I complain? He submits to the exercises and treatments without argument, although they leave him in pain. If he needs to find relief in Catilius, or other ancient writers, then he must be allowed to."

"He is not neglecting you?"

"No. We have a difference of opinion over something right now, and it is causing a certain tension between us. We will resolve it, do not worry," she added. "It is just Cillian being self-sacrificing, once again."

I didn't press her. She'd tell me, if she wanted. Or he would. Some days after our aborted *xache* game, I'd gone to talk to him. He had been reading—Lena was right, books were his occupation and his solace now—but he'd put the volume down to greet me with genuine welcome.

"It is your move," he said. I studied the *xache* board, seeing what he'd done, and that whatever move I made, I was left in a vulnerable position. How long had it taken him to see where to place his piece?

"You've had days to think about this," I complained. "Do I get the same?"

"No. Consider it practice for your work as a *toscaire*, once the Procurator returns. You will need to weigh your moves quickly then." He'd sounded serious. I raised an eyebrow, considered the board again, and made my choice.

Since then we had continued the game, Cillian inviting me to make my move almost daily now. The outcome was still uncertain, and that told me much.

In the past, he had usually beaten me in half-a-dozen moves, or even fewer.

Druise came in, carrying a tray with jugs of wine and water. "You needed more," he said.

"I could have done that," Lena said. "You are Cillian's aide, Druise, not mine."

"You both drink the wine," he said. "And so do I, sometimes. Sorley, you are wanted in the *Princip*'s workroom. Bring your list of harbours, I was to tell you."

The commander of the northern fleet must have arrived. The ships had been out, the calm, mild winter allowing them to patrol the coast at a time when it would have been next to impossible, most years. I went to my study, found my papers, and presented myself to Casyn.

He was looking at a map with another man, younger than I had expected, dark haired, lean, with lines around his blue eyes that spoke of hours spent in sea light.

"Lord Sorley," Casyn said, "may I present Dern, commander of our northern fleet? He knows the waters between here and the Sterre well; I will leave the two of you to discuss harbours."

Dern? Where had I heard that name recently? "Captain of *Skua*?" I asked.

"I am. How did you know that?"

"Lena mentioned it, not very long ago," I told him.

"In all that has happened," Casyn said, smiling, "I

had almost forgotten those weeks you spent at Tirvan. An oversight. Lord Sorley is a close friend of Lena's, Dern. He will give you news of her, as well as of Linrathe's harbours. Other duties require my attention, but this room is yours."

"How is Lena?" Dern asked, as soon as Casyn had left us. He gestured to the chairs. "Shall we sit, Lord Sorley?"

"Sorley," I said. "Lena is well, now." I hesitated. "I don't know what you last heard of her."

"I knew of her exile, and return, with a new form of archery, and that using it she killed Fritjof," he said, a man used to delivering concise reports. "Beyond that, very little. We have been on patrol almost ever since. Was she injured at the Taiva?"

"Not her," I said. "Her partner. The Emperor's son, Cillian."

"Didn't he die, alongside the Emperor?"

"No. He was very badly wounded, but somehow he survived. His recovery is certain now, but it has been a strain on Lena. In part because their child will be born in a few weeks."

"I remember her as resourceful, and a leader, even at eighteen," he said. "I would like to see her, if possible."

"I imagine she would be glad to," I said. I liked him already, an instinctive reaction. "If you know the waters as well as Casyn says you do, our business won't take long. I'd guess you are using all the harbours the *Teannasach* has suggested already. I could take you to see her, afterwards, if you have time."

"Then shall we get to work?" He eyed me. "May I say, Sorley, you are not what I expected in Linrathe's official envoy?"

"You thought someone older, austere and precise?" I said, grinning. "I am a musician, Dern, not a diplomat. But war and its aftermath ask many things of us we did not expect, and I am in this role because I was party to the treaties signed in Casil. A signatory, for Linrathe. It is a long story," I added, at his look of astonishment.

"One I would like to hear, someday," he said. "Shall we get to work?"

As I had guessed, there was little to discuss. Dern knew the coves, and which harbours could take the ships, and where the fresh water was. He even pointed out two locations where shifting sands made access impossible now. I rolled up my map. "Come and see Lena," I said.

I knocked at their door before opening it. Lena had long ago told me not to wait, but I always let them know it was me by my triple rap. Lena looked up from where she sat with Cillian and Dagney, and for a moment I thought she was irritated by the interruption. Then her eyes moved past me, to Dern, and her face changed.

"Dern?"

"Lena." The moment felt awkward.

"Dern is commander of the northern fleet," I said.

"We have been meeting about harbours, and I remembered you had mentioned his name, Lena."

"If I am intruding?" he asked.

"Not at all," Cillian said. "You have simply surprised us. Forgive me for not rising, but it is still difficult for me." He saluted Dern. "Commander, I am Cillian, Major and adjutant to the *Princip*, currently on leave. May I introduce the Lady Dagney of the *Ti'ach na Perras*?" So very formal. Why?

Dern said the appropriate things, and as Dagney asked a polite question Lena almost visibly took command of herself and stood up. "You did take me by surprise," she said. "I am so pleased to see you, Dern. I asked about *Skua*, before the Taiva, but no one knew where you were."

"North," he said, "almost to Varsland, among the islands. We owe you the victory, I understand."

"I killed Fritjof," she said, "but there was more to the victory than that. I did what I was trained for, nothing more."

He heard the unspoken message in her tone, responding only with a nod. "Garth?" she asked.

"On Leste," he said. "Did you not know? He knows their customs and the language so well. He is one of Bren's adjutants." Lena smiled then, relief evident on her face.

"I have not seen him since Karst," she said. "I wonder if Maya knows where he is?"

"Messengers ride to the Eastern Fort, and Casilla

is on the way," Cillian said. "A letter can be sent." He had not offered wine. "As one can be to Leste, if you wish."

"Perhaps." She smiled at Dern again. "Thank you for the news, Dern."

"Had I known you were here, and worrying, I would have made sure you knew before," he said. "I must return to the harbour. Lady Dagney, Major. No, Lord Sorley, I know my way," he added, as I made a move to accompany him. Lena did walk with him to the door. They exchanged a few quiet words, Cillian's eyes on them the entire time. I glanced at Dagney. She made a tiny negative movement with her head. What had I brought Dern into? Whatever it was, his presence had not helped.

"Sorley," Dagney said, as soon as Lena had closed the door, "I have the beginnings of a headache. Will you walk with me out-of-doors? The light fades, and I do not see as well as I used to. I would appreciate your arm."

Outside in the dusk, I gave Dagney my arm. Her need for it was not feigned, although I was sure her reasons for taking me from the room were. "Are you going to tell me?" I asked.

"It is not mine to tell," she replied. We walked a few steps.

"Is it serious? Lena said a little while ago they disagreed over something, but it was only Cillian's tendency to self-sacrifice again, and not to worry."

"It will be serious, if Cillian does not see sense within a few weeks."

"Within a few weeks? You mean before the baby is born?"

"Yes," she said. She was bound by her oath to answer any direct question honestly, and both of us knew it. I framed my next words carefully.

"Is he risking their child's legitimacy in Linrathe?"

"I do not understand how he can," she said, frustration breaking through in her voice. "He swore he would not make any child live through what he did, and yet he is baulking now at the marriage he asked me here to perform. He will not tie her to him, he says."

"She is vowed to him, and he to her," I said. "I held those vows for them, Dagney, before they told them to each other. What difference can a ceremony make?"

"He has told her she is free of that vow to him. She says she is not, and never will be. I have tried to mediate, but—" Her hand tightened on my arm. "Sorley, they are breaking my heart. All Perras wanted, all I want, is Cillian home again, at the *Ti'ach* where he belongs. He is making that impossible."

"It is all he wanted, too," I said slowly. "He told Lena that, before the Taiva. The *Ti'ach*, and her there with him. And me, he said. What has changed?"

"His injuries," she said, and words Lena had

spoken weeks before came back to me. *He may never walk again, or make love.*

"Oh, gods," I said. "And I brought Dern to her? There was something between them once, don't you think? And she asked about Garth, and I know they were lovers, and so does Cillian."

"Maya, too, was mentioned. Lena has told me what happened in the Kurzemë camp, and that she cannot ever see herself with another man. Cillian, with precise logic, argues that she does not preclude a woman, and he will not rob her of that comfort. Nor of the chance to have another child, if some day she wishes to."

"What does Gnaius say?"

"That he does not know, and only time will tell. But time we do not have, Sorley."

We walked towards the outer walls. A white owl perched, staring down into the fields beyond. At our approach, it lifted off on silent wings, gliding into the dark. I looked up at the first stars, thinking about a conversation with Talyn. "Can you marry them without vows of physical fidelity?"

She stopped. "What are you suggesting, Sorley?"

"I cannot speak for the *torpari*, Dagney," I began, "but among the *Härren* of Sorham, marriage is about joining lands together, or strengthening trade alliances. Vows of faithfulness are made, but no one really expects those to be kept, certainly not by the man. And not always by the women, once the heirs are safely born. Will you tell me I'm wrong?"

"You are not," she admitted.

"Then why cannot Lena and Cillian be married without making those promises? Is it a requirement of the ceremony?"

"Not that I have ever been told. It is simply the tradition."

"And what is traditional about a Linrathan *scáeli* marrying two citizens of the southern Empire, a land which has not held a wedding in several hundred years?"

"You," she said, "have learned quite a lot in your time with Cillian, haven't you? You were never so devious when you were at the *Ti'ach*."

"There wasn't the need."

"Not that you saw. If they agree, I will do this. Shall I speak to them, or will you?"

"I will," I said.

I escorted Dagney back to her room. Cillian would be expecting me, I thought. He was alone, a book in his hand. "You asked, of course," he said.

"Of course." I poured myself wine. He shook his head when I held up the flask. "Where is Lena?"

"She went for a walk. Gnaius tells her it is good for her and the baby, and we needed time apart."

I sat down across from him. "Cillian, you are being a fool."

"I am not," he said firmly. "How can I tie Lena to me?"

"Is that not her choice?"

"One she will regret."

"You dare say that to me?" I asked, anger flaring. I was angry so often now. "Do you think Lena less constant than I?"

"No," he said. "No, I do not. But you have Druisius. I am not questioning her love, Sorley. But I am—not a man, and may never be again. How can that be fair to her?"

"This is not just about you and Lena," I said. "There is the child."

"Who in this country will be acknowledged as mine by a declaration."

"But not in Linrathe." I held up a hand, forestalling his next utterance. "Cillian, there is a simple solution. You are not arguing that you do not love each other, nor that you are not vowed to each other, only that to swear an oath of bodily fidelity is unreasonable, given the circumstance. Am I right?"

"You are."

"Then don't swear that oath. Dagney will marry you without it." I hesitated. "I expect you can swear fidelity if you like, but not Lena, if that suits you better."

His eyes narrowed. "Dagney will do this?"

"She has told me she will."

I watched him considering the proposal. "Whose idea was this?"

"Mine," I admitted.

"We are making a *toscaire* of you after all," he said. "I need to think about this, Sorley, and there are things I must say to Lena."

"Shall I find her, and ask her to return?"

"If you would. Thank you, *mo charaidh*."

I drained my wine cup. In the corridor, I leaned against the wall. I needed a moment to regain my own composure. Why was I shaking?

I had suggested to Dagney she marry them without an oath of bodily fidelity, to overcome Cillian's reluctance and ensure the child was legitimate. But had that been my only motive? Cillian would never break an oath. Had I hoped not just Lena would forgo that vow, but that he would too, leaving the possibility that, someday, he might—?

I forced my mind away from the thought. What a fool I was. I had to mould what I felt for Cillian back into what I had believed it had become in Casil, and what I had claimed to Dagney: a brotherly love. Unless I did, what future could there be for us?

CHAPTER 14

A RIDER ARRIVED very early the next morning, to announce that Decanius would reach the fort by midday, and expected his rooms warmed, the baths reserved, and that after he was suitably refreshed, he would meet with the *Princip*. Or so Casyn told me, with such a look of intermingled horror and resignation that I could not help laughing.

"Will you join us?" he asked. "After what you and Cillian said about Randall, I want your translation, not just his."

"With pleasure," I said, as drily as I could, which made Casyn laugh too. Accordingly, I cancelled my afternoon language classes and presented myself at the appropriate hour.

"Lord Sorley," Decanius said. "I see no need for your presence."

"But the *Princip* does," I told him. "Randall na Asgaill can return now to the duties he was sent here to perform, and which I had taken over so as not to delay the officers here learning your language, Procurator. I will translate now."

He didn't like it, that was obvious, but Randall was not his to command. He wasn't really mine, either, but I was senior in years, and Linrathe's appointed envoy. "Randall may stay for this meeting," I added, "but after today he must return to teaching."

"Very well," Decanius said. "*Princip*, the *mensores* have completed their surveys in the south. There is much good land for vineyards and grain, and to the west salterns, and closer to the mountains, fine grazing. We will discuss the division of this land into estates, and the management of those estates to feed both this land and to send surpluses to Casil."

"The salterns and much of the land of which you speak are held by the villages," Casyn said. "They manage them, and have fed themselves and our army for generations."

"But now it must feed both villages and armies here and in other parts of the Eastern Empire," Decanius said. "Different techniques are needed. And the product of salterns, by our laws, goes first to the Eastern Empire. Casil alone needs much salt, and our armies as well. I will be overseeing that personally."

"Of course," Casyn said, managing to keep his voice level. "Shall we consult a map about these lands you wish to divide, Procurator?"

By the time the discussion ended, my neck and shoulders ached with tension. Casyn smashed his fist on the table as soon as the door closed behind Decanius. "He cares not at all for how this land has been held for generations," he said. "He will reduce the villages to the equivalent of your *torps*, Sorley, but with his Casilani friends in place of your nobles." Anger roughened his voice. "How did Turlo let this happen? I place no blame on Cillian; I can see such an arrangement would seem normal to him, being Linrathan. But Turlo should have objected."

"It was never discussed," I said, "or not while I was there, at least. But we read Cillian's translations of the treaties, *Princip*, and you know it is not included, not in this detail. But Casil's laws take precedence in your agreement, and that has a broad interpretation."

"We are being treated as a conquered people."

"Forgive me, Casyn," I said hesitantly. "I know very little of your country's history, but this land was a province of Casil once before, wasn't it?"

"Yes. Many generations past."

"And your laws derive from Casil's, assumedly?" A vague memory was stirring, too vague to mention to Casyn.

"Many of them. Those governing the army, certainly. But after the assembly that divided men's lives from women's, and created the women's villages, the laws governing those developed separately. How, I cannot tell you."

"Are there records?" I asked.

"If there are, they are at the Eastern Fort. Old Jereme would have known, and Colm, but they are both dead. Where is Birel, with the wine?" He got up to open the door to the adjoining room, calling his aide's name.

"Will you excuse me, *Princip*?" I asked. "I should speak with Randall about the language classes."

"Yes, certainly," he said, head bent again over a map. "Tell the guard I am not to be disturbed, if you will."

Randall, I was told, was still with Decanius. I left word with the Procurator's guard that I needed to see my countryman, either this evening or tomorrow morning. I walked down the corridor, rotating my shoulders to try to ease the tension in them. I needed the baths.

And why not? I turned into the corridor that led to the bath house. I didn't need a cloak for the brief distance outside, not this winter. Steam escaped from its ventilation shafts: unlike Casil's baths, the water of the hot pool here came naturally from underground.

No one was there but the attendant: with Decanius back, probably the assumption had been made that he would claim this time for himself. I soaked, trying for a while to remember what it was

I knew about the laws of this land, and Casil's. The memory eluded me, although I was sure Turlo had been the one who had told me. On Irmgard's ship, maybe?

Inevitably my thoughts took me to finding Cillian and Lena so unexpectedly, so impossibly, in that empty, distant land, the chances of that meeting infinitesimal. But it had been that tiny possibility that had sent me east with Turlo, an admission I had never made—nor would ever make—to anyone. From the moment I had heard, horrified, of Cillian's exile, I had promised myself to search for him. How, I had no idea. Until I met Turlo in the foothills of the Durrains, and heard his plans to find the route east to Casil.

I had not done what I had been sent to Sorham to do, to see if there were men who would oppose Fritjof. My loyalty had not been to Linrathe, but to my heart. I had abandoned my land in war for a hopeless dream.

Yet, if I hadn't—could Fritjof have been defeated, otherwise? Without me, to convince Irmgard in Marái'sta of the need, we would never have been on her ship. And without—what? the hand of a god?— that had brought Cillian and Lena to the riverbank at the precise moment our ship passed, we would never have obtained Casil's aid. Perhaps I had been meant to choose to go east, not north.

And perhaps I was justifying what I had done, and nothing more.

I left the baths, my aches barely alleviated, deciding to eat at the senior commons. Someone would claim me as guest; preferably someone who would leave me alone. I scanned the interior of the room, not yet full, finding Talyn. I indicated her to the steward; he went to ask. She turned, nodded to the steward, and beckoned me over.

"I'm leaving shortly," she said.

"That's fine. I'm not in the mood for company, really."

"Decanius? I heard he was back."

"Yes. Full of plans to oversee salt production, among other things."

"Enriching himself in the process, no doubt," she murmured. I moved to a small table, welcoming the wine the steward brought. I was half-way through my meal when he came over to me again.

"You are being asked for, Lord Sorley," he said. "Your countryman, Randall."

"Should I go out to him?" I asked. "Or may he join me?"

"I shouldn't allow it, as you're a guest." I knew him slightly, outside of this role; he diced with Druisius, and sometimes I joined my lover in the soldiers' commons. Musicians were welcome almost everywhere. He gave me a wink. "But seeing it's you, I'll make an exception."

He ushered Randall over. I offered wine, and food; he accepted the first. We chatted for a few minutes about the unseasonable weather, and the ride north. "I have four groups of officers I have been teaching," I told him, bringing the conversation around to business. "Shall we go to my workroom to review the lessons?"

That took nearly an hour. When we had finished, I asked, casually, "Did you find it difficult to translate the old records at the Eastern Fort?"

"Very few of the records the Procurator looked at were old," he said. "He was more interested in maps, and meeting with his surveyors, and the captain newly arrived from Casil. I was rarely needed, so I did what the *Teannasach* sent me to do, and taught Casilan to the officers there."

"He did not consult the tax records, and documents on land ownership?"

"A few. But only when we were first there." Some instinct told me he was being evasive.

"I see. You said a ship arrived from Casil?" I supposed they must now, and their first docking would always be the Eastern Fort.

"Aye. The captain had records from Casil that interested the Procurator. Something to do with the army, but that is all I know."

"Well, thank you, Randall," I said. "I will not keep you, after your long ride today."

He stood. "Good night, Lord Sorley." I turned back to my papers, tidying them.

"Leave the door," I heard Druise say. I looked up. He didn't come in, just stood in the opening. "Cillian wants you," he told me, once Randall had left. The peremptory statement irritated me, even though the words were probably Druise's, not Cillian's.

"I wish," I muttered, regretting the words immediately. I'd promised Druise. But he just grinned.

"Cillian would like your company," he amended. "Although," he added, as I stood to go, "the other could be possible, too."

"When cows fly," I said in my dialect. At Druise's questioning look, I translated.

"We would say 'when a mule foals'. He is in his study."

I was still vaguely out of sorts when I knocked on the study door. Too many meetings, too many problems to solve, too little music. I hadn't brought my *ladhar,* though. Cillian was studying the *xache* board; we were part-way through a game.

He greeted me with a smile, and my irritation receded. "*Mo charaidh*, thank you for coming."

"Did you want to play?"

"Perhaps later. I proposed your idea to Lena."

"And?"

"She sees the sense."

"She isn't the one who needs to," I said. "Do you?"

"You are sure Dagney will do this? Marriage vows that do not speak of fidelity?"

"Haven't you asked her?" He shook his head. I sighed in exasperation. "Yes, I am sure."

"Lena and I talked late into the night," he said, his

eyes reflecting candlelight, "of all the reasons I have been reluctant to commit us to the traditional vows." He studied me across the table. "May I ask something?"

"Of course."

"Do you have half-brothers or sisters? Other than by your father's second wife, I mean."

"On other estates, almost certainly. On our own *torp,* no. Gundar has his own code of behaviour. What does this have to do with you and Lena?"

"Something she told me made me realize I need to—rearrange my ideas. A lesson for me in the danger of making assumptions. I have therefore been considering what I know of marriage in Linrathe and Sorham. Very little, it appears."

"Why would you? You grew up at the *Ti'ach.*"

"So what is marriage for, in your view?"

"For the landholders? To unite property, create alliances, raise children," I said.

"A form of politics, then?"

"Among the nobles, yes. But also for day-to-day companionship, and shared responsibility. And laughter, and enjoyment and comfort. If the pairing is a good one, it is like true harmony in song."

"Always the musician," he said. "But harmony is not disturbed by the occasional grace note?"

"Dagney," I said, "would be pleased. You did pay attention to her lessons."

He smiled a little at that. "I am decided, Sorley, although there is one barrier yet. I will not marry

Lena while the poppy clouds my mind. I have spoken to Gnaius. Tomorrow we will begin to reduce it. Two weeks to free me from it completely, he says."

Two weeks. "The child is due when?"

"She was conceived on midsummer's day," he said. "Of that Lena is sure."

"You may be holding the ceremony in the birthing room," I said.

"First babies are often late," he said, "or so I am told, and choose to believe." He shifted, wincing.

"I hope you are right." I would offer him the *li'ítho* at another time, I thought. "Are you in pain, Cillian?"

"Not more than usual. Druise will bring the drug soon, the last full dose. I have told Lena, and now I tell you: stay away from me, until I am fully free of it."

"Cillian," I protested, "will not music help?"

"It may. But Druisius can play for me. This will be an unpleasant process, I understand. I may do and say things I would regret you witnessing."

"As you wish," I said. What else could I say? "But if you need me, send for me."

"I will. I am afraid I do not have the concentration for *xache, mo charaidh*. Will you leave me to my books?"

Walking back to my room, I thought about my own words: *companionship, and shared responsibility; laughter, and enjoyment and comfort.* Wasn't this what I had with Druise?

"He has told you?" Druise asked, drinking a last cup of wine before bed. "He goes back to the infirmary tomorrow. Stay away, Sorley, until you are told to come. He does not want you to see him as he will be. Neither you, nor Lena."

"So he said," I told him. "You have seen this before?"

"A friend. Another soldier. But no Gnaius, to do this gently. He was put in a cell and left for ten days. Some of us brought water, and food, and tried to help." He shrugged. "He made it through, and lived. But the poppy was too easy to get, and his desire too great. He died from it, in a way: stabbed one night in an alley for his money, while searching for an apothecary."

"Druise, thank you. For doing all you have, for Cillian." We did talk of Cillian in our room—almost impossible not to, given Druise's responsibilities. But only for a while, and only as we sat by the fire reviewing the day. The bed was for us alone.

"He wants to be free of it. My friend did not. It is all the difference." He put down the empty cup. "I will not see you, *amané*, for two weeks. Maybe a little less."

"Not at all?"

"Briefly. So perhaps we could leave these chairs? I must sleep, but not yet."

CHAPTER 15

DRUISE, EXHAUSTED AND GRIM, sat with Lena and me in her rooms. Grey with fatigue, he had accepted wine gratefully. "Gnaius is with him," he had told us, when he'd appeared unexpectedly.

"Is he…" Lena's voice trailed off. "There is no danger, is there?"

"No," Druise said, "only it is hard. Harder maybe than Cillian imagined."

I went to stand behind him, massaging his neck and shoulders. I wasn't particularly good at this, but I needed to do something. "Do you have time for the baths?"

"Harder how?" Lena asked, at the same moment. "Is the pain very bad, without the poppy?"

"Maybe the baths," Druise agreed. "Not the pain, Lena. Gnaius gives him other drugs for that. It is what he sees, what comes from his mind. Bad memories. Things he has done, that he does not forgive himself for."

Lena stared at nothing, shaking her head slightly. "I wish I knew what haunts him," she murmured. "He would never tell me. But there is something, isn't there? He said once he didn't believe redemption was possible, not for living people."

We had spoken of this in Casil, I remembered. "How can he have done anything that terrible?"

"Terrible to him," Druise said. "Maybe not to you." In the hall outside the room, I heard voices, and heavy feet. I turned, frowning. The door swung open. Four soldiers—all Casilani—marched in. One was a sergeant.

"Druisius, soldier of Casil," the sergeant said. "You are under arrest for desertion."

"No," I said. "There is some mistake. Druisius is assigned to the Major Cillian, on General Turlo's orders."

"This soldier deserted after the battle at the Taiva," the officer said. "I have my orders."

"Orders from whom?" Lena demanded.

"The Procurator." My hand was still on Druise's shoulder.

"Address me properly, Sergeant," she snapped.

"Lieutenant," he said. "Do not try to stop us. Lord Sorley, move aside."

"Do not argue," Druise said softly. He stood up.

"No," I said, trying to shield him.

"Sorley." Druise's voice was firm. "Tell Gnaius." He pushed past me, allowing two of the soldiers to take his arms, none too gently.

"Your name, Sergeant?" Lena demanded. He told her. "Where are you taking Druisius?"

"The cells, Lieutenant. Take him," he said to his men. They marched out. I took a step to follow, but Lena stopped me.

"No, Sorley. Go to the infirmary, as Druise said. Tell Gnaius. I will find Casyn. But tell me first: did he desert?"

I came with Lena, without permission. "Yes," I said. "But Turlo knew. He said it wouldn't matter, that we would just say the transfer to the Empire's troops was made on the field, without written confirmation."

"Maybe. But think, Sorley. To arrest a senior officer's aide so peremptorily, when that senior officer is signatory to the treaty, and the *Princip*'s nephew? Decanius is making a statement about who has power now, and he is using Druisius to do it."

"Oh, gods," I said. "Is there a message here to Linrathe, too? All Wall's End knows Druise is my partner."

"Very likely. Now go. Gnaius needs to know, and he will not, if you stand there."

She had reached for her officer's insignia as she spoke. Off duty, she didn't wear it; it lay on the sideboard beside Cillian's. "Sorley," she said sharply, pinning it on, "Go."

The cadet at the infirmary door did not want to let me in. "I must," I said, trying not to shout. "I must see Gnaius. I have an important message for him. The *Princip* is aware."

The last might be a lie, but I didn't care. The girl stepped aside. I entered the antechamber, turning left to what had been Cillian's room before. Gnaius was just coming out. "You should not be here," he said.

"Druisius has been arrested," I said.

His eyes widened, but he said nothing, only closed the door quietly behind him. "Cillian is sleeping, but only because I gave him valerian," he murmured. "A light sleep, easily disturbed. Come over here, and keep your voice down."

I told him what had happened, as quickly as I could. "I cannot leave Cillian," he said, his brow furrowed.

"Could I stay with him?"

"No. You do not know what to do, and there is no time to teach you. And…" He hesitated. "What Cillian says to us—you must understand that he has little control, and he tells us things he would not otherwise. Some of it, Lord Sorley, concerns you. As his physician, I cannot allow him to see you; I would fear the effects on the balance of his mind." He turned to a table. "I will write a note to Decanius. Wait outside, please. I will not take long."

I waited silently by the cadet, confusion and fear warring in my mind. Fear for Druise, and confusion at Gnaius's words. What could Cillian be saying?

That he had turned my advances down? That wasn't a secret, not among us, and surely we had moved beyond regret.

Staring down the corridor, I let myself remember. He'd taken me aside on the river, one early morning, and we'd walked a long way from the ship before we stopped. 'Sorley,' he'd said, 'I have made many mistakes in my life. One has caused you great pain. I regret that.' I'd interrupted, with some disavowal or dismissal, but he'd gone on. 'Loving Lena has made me understand.' He'd put a hand on my shoulder, then. 'I wish I had known.'

I had begun to cry, trying to hide the tears and failing. The hand on my shoulder had moved to my back, and I had turned to him. He had held me gently, not speaking. I hadn't let it go on for too long; pride made me step away. The glitter of tears in his eyes had surprised me.

'But there is no going back,' he'd said. 'Can you forgive me, and be my friend?'

Of course I had said I would: friendship was preferable to nothing. And in the weeks in Casil and the ship home, we had been friends, and I had thought myself content. Had Cillian sensed my anger and confusion this winter? Had I inadvertently resurrected his guilt and regret?

I couldn't make sense of it. And maybe there was none: maybe the poppy twisted memories and thought, and what Cillian was telling Gnaius and

Druise was nonsensical. I'd talk to Druise about it, someday.

If he was here to talk to. Fear surged again. I began to pace. Where was Gnaius? He appeared a minute or two later, a sealed note in his hand. "Take this to the *Princip*. If the Procurator is to be found, ask them both to attend me, if they would."

Casyn, Lena with him, was in his workroom. I handed him Gnaius's note. "I have spoken to Randall," he said. "He believes the captain that Decanius met with at the Eastern Fort had brought records from Casil, names of missing men. I have seen how carefully they keep their lists and tallies, and the god forbid they allot pay improperly. Druisius's name must have been on that list."

"But we can still argue the transfer was made in the field," I said again.

"No," Lena said. "If he is listed as missing, then his commander knows no transfer was made."

I swore. "What is the punishment?"

Casyn looked up. "Surely you know?"

"No."

I saw the answer in his eyes before he spoke. "Death."

Lena reached out to me, but I turned away, staring at the wall. "There must be a solution," I insisted. Fear made my voice sharp.

"A temporary one, yes," Casyn said. "Sergeant!" Birel appeared almost immediately. "My compliments to the Procurator," he said, "with a request from the physician Gnaius that we both join him immediately. Lord Sorley will accompany you to translate, but here is the physician's note, and my signature."

He touched Lena's shoulder. "You must stay here. I can think of no reason to have you join us, and your presence will inflame Decanius."

The Procurator came with bad grace, but Gnaius held a senior rank in the Casilani army, and his note had made it clear, I guessed, that he could not leave the infirmary. Gnaius took us all into an inner room, well away from where Cillian was being treated.

"Physician?" Decanius said. "What requires my presence?" Posturing, I thought. *He knows.*

"Procurator, *Princip*, you have had a man I need arrested," Gnaius said. His voice was quiet, almost questioning. "Druisius, his name is."

"A deserter," Decanius said.

"That may be," Gnaius replied. "But I have spent many hours training this man, and I need him just now, for another week. I request his return. You may, of course, send guards. I will take responsibility for him, as my rank allows."

"You have many medics."

"But the treatment I need Druisius to assist with is a delicate one. One from which I will learn to the benefit of all Casil's army. I will ensure your cooperation will be made clear to the Empress."

Decanius rubbed his chin. "You will take full responsibility?"

"Of course."

"A week, you say?"

"Or a day or two more. No longer."

"Then—" His eyes flicked to Casyn. "If you agree, *Princip*. I want it clear," he said, turning back to Gnaius, "that if anything goes wrong, the *Princip* and I both agreed to the deserter's stay of execution."

"Of course," Gnaius said again. "*Princip*?"

"I agree, if you believe only he has the skills you require," Casyn said, through me. Gnaius smiled, blandly.

"Thank you both. I would appreciate it if Druisius could return immediately. I will need him very soon."

I sank into a chair in Casyn's workroom. Birel handed me wine, unwatered. "The physician is also a diplomat," Casyn said, sipping his own wine.

"They must be, I should think," Lena said. "But you say Decanius was quick to include you in the decision?"

Casyn laughed, cynically. "Only to ensure any blame would be shared. But we also know now that Decanius curries the Empress's favour, not just his uncle's, which might be useful. At least we have gained some time."

I did not sleep that night, even though Gnaius sent the cadet with a note to tell me Druise was back with him. 'A few bruises, nothing more,' the physician wrote.

I paced, picking up and putting down my *ladhar* a dozen times. The flask of *fuisce* grew lighter, and with it, my remorse. We—Cillian and I—had offered Druise the chance to accompany us west. To war, yes, and so there had always been risk. But somehow death in battle and execution for desertion weren't the same.

But, my muddled mind said, how can he have deserted? He'd fought with his regiment at the Taiva; the battle and the war were won when he left his fellow soldiers to support Lena. And Callan had signed the treaty weeks before. He was still a soldier, assigned his current post by a general of the Empire's army, and the Empire's army now was Casil's.

Did the argument make sense? I didn't know. I wasn't a soldier. But it gave me hope, and it was something to think about, something other than the thing I didn't want to examine, the other reason behind my guilt. As much as I wanted to deny it, when Casyn had told me the punishment, a voice in my mind, insidious and unwelcome, had whispered: *then you would have no choice to make.*

I dozed briefly, sodden with *fuisce*, just as the sky began to lighten. I woke after an hour or so, my head pounding and my stomach roiling. Sitting up was a mistake. I vomited into the chamber pot, several times, and then I sat with my back against the bed, waiting for the room to stop spinning.

Eventually I kept some water down, and managed to wash and dress. Shaving was not possible, my hand far too unsteady. I made my way to Cillian and Lena's rooms, and weakly rapped three times.

"Oh, Sorley," Lena said when she opened the door to me. "Sit down. Tea?"

"No. Nothing."

"*Fuisce*," she said, sniffing. "I shouldn't have let you leave."

"There's only one bed."

"So? Have we not shared a cot before?"

"I had a thought," I said.

"I'm surprised you could," she said. "Before the *fuisce*?"

I shook my head, and wished I hadn't. "No. During...and so it might not make sense." I told her my thinking, about how Druise couldn't have deserted. She listened, biting her lip.

"Maybe," she said. "Casyn will know. He said to come to him, whenever we were ready. Are you?"

"Yes. As long as there isn't food."

Casyn gave me a sympathetic look, and heard me out, but at the end of my explanation he shook his head. "The argument is not without merit, Sorley.

But I doubt Decanius will accept it: Casil's military laws are harsh. But it is worth trying, if he rejects Gnaius's idea. The physician came to see me very early this morning."

"Which is?"

"I bribe him," he said simply.

"With what? Doesn't he think everything is his for the taking?" Lena asked.

"Perhaps bribe is the wrong word," Casyn said. "I agree to certain practices that will enrich him, practices that in truth divert money from Casil's coffers to his own purse."

"Does not that endanger you?" I asked, "if Casil discovers the fraud?"

"It is a possibility," he agreed. "But one that has little chance of detection, because the man who oversees such things in Casil is Decanius's kinsman, Quintus."

"You would do this," I asked, "for Druisius? One soldier, not even of your land?"

"I will do this because Decanius is going to divert taxes to his own use whether I agree or not. Also, it suits me to have the Procurator think he has cowed me into submitting to his authority," Casyn said. "And because Druisius matters to you, and to Cillian and Lena, and too many we love have died." He stood up. "Go to the baths, Sorley. Lieutenant, you will stay with me, please: there are many facets of this plan to work out, and Michan cannot be part of it."

I soaked a long time, and let the attendant shave me. I felt somewhat better, physically. Soup and bread, tentatively approached, stayed in my stomach, and once I was sure of that I went back to see what Lena and Casyn had devised. I stopped at the infirmary first, but a large guardsman at the door told me convincingly I was not allowed inside. I wondered what he'd say if I told him I had come for a remedy for my uncertain stomach, but decided not to try my luck.

"Decanius has agreed to meet with me in an hour, with you to translate," Casyn told me. "I have sent Lena for food and a rest, as she must be our scribe."

He told me the plan, and what he had to offer. "I am taking nothing from the women's villages that the Procurator will not claim as Casil's due," he said, "from what he has informed me of already." He looked at me critically. "I am glad to see you are shaven. May I suggest you change into your formal clothes?"

"Am I not just your translator?"

"It will not hurt to remind Decanius that you are also the ears and voice of Linrathe. Whatever they will ask of your country, Sorley, when they choose to ask it, having even the slightest sway over the Procurator might be to your advantage."

I couldn't argue. I went back my room, both relieved and embarrassed to see it had been cleaned. I'd have to make my appreciation known to the orderly. When I returned to Casyn's workroom, Lena was present, and Birel, the latter laying out writing supplies on a smaller table against the wall.

"Is there anything else, *Princip*?" he asked.

"Not if there is water and wine," Casyn said. "Thank you, Sergeant."

His soldier-servant didn't leave. The two men regarded each other. "Be careful, Casyn," Birel said. "You are needed still."

"I will be."

A smile half-formed on Birel's lips, and disappeared. He saluted and left us. A few minutes later, Decanius's scribe knocked, and the two men came in.

"What is she doing here?" Decanius demanded, looking at Lena. "A pregnant woman?" His lip curled.

"The lieutenant," Casyn said firmly, "is my scribe today. My adjutant has other duties."

Decanius scowled. "At least she is not at this table," he muttered. He chose a chair. "What is it you so urgently need to discuss, *Princip*?"

"I have been giving thought to an appropriate residence for you, Procurator. You cannot wish to reside in the rooms you were assigned here permanently, surely?"

"Well, no," Decanius said, looking both surprised and pleased. "This fort is far from what I am accustomed to."

"I thought as much," Casyn said. "Coming from Casil, you must find these northern lands both cold and damp, do you not?"

"It is damp in Casil in the winter, but not this cold," Decanius said. "And of course our heating is better. What did you have in mind? I did ask the *mensores* to consider this, as they mapped the land."

I handed Casyn the map that, rolled, lay beside me. We spread it out, weighting the corners. "Here," Casyn said, pointing to land between the Eastern Fort and Casilla. Decanius's eyes widened.

"Is not that a residence of a retired officer?"

"It is. But the officer could be persuaded to let you have it. The house is of sufficient quality that you should be comfortable there until you can build something more fitting your position, Procurator." Casyn sat back, letting Decanius study the map.

"There are vineyards?"

"Established ones. The wine is very good, by our standards."

"I would bring a wine-maker from Casil. Are there slaves?"

"Yes. Only male, of course."

"And metals?"

"Copper. The mines are on this headland here." Casyn pointed.

Decanius leaned back in his chair. "I have one concern," he said. "Shall we ask our scribes to stop writing, *Princip*?" When pens were down, he continued. "I would, of course, need to build a villa that honoured myself and my family in Casil. My salary as Procurator, while generous, is insufficient for that purpose."

"Have you a solution?" Casyn inquired neutrally. "I too will have payments to make, to ensure these lands can be yours."

The inner door opened. Casyn looked up, frowning. Birel came in, a wine flask on a tray in his hands. "My apologies, *Princip*. I remembered I had not put out the best wine." He put it down and slipped away, pulling the door closed behind him.

"A cup would be welcome," Decanius said. I rose to pour, something nagging at me. Something missing...a sound I should have heard. I poured two cups, put the flask down. It clicked against the metal tray.

I served the wine cups, then reached for the water jug. As I did, I glanced at the inner door, sure now of what I hadn't heard: the click of its latch. It stood ajar, the tiniest crack.

Decanius began talking again. "The taxation rates on certain commodities are my decision. That I keep a percentage of the rates I set, for the responsibility of managing those commodities, is common practice, *Princip*. An unspoken agreement between Casil and its provincial administrators, you understand."

"Is it?" Casyn said. "What commodities might you consider for this arrangement?"

"Salt, for one," Decanius said. "It is in great demand, and this coastal land has much opportunity for its production. A percentage of its taxes would quickly enrich me, and," he cleared his throat, "perhaps you too, *Princip*, if other arrangements of this sort could be made?"

"You are forgetting something, Procurator." We all turned. In the frame of the inner door, Cillian leaned on a cane, his face drawn, his hands trembling. He wore grey and white, his court clothes from Casil, although they hung on him. Lena made a sound, but she didn't move.

"Cillian!" Casyn said. "Major, what are you doing here?"

Decanius looked at Cillian, his face cold. He said something in a language I did not recognize. It sounded like *zinkolo*.

Cillian replied in what I assumed was the same language. "I can repeat that, if you like," he added, in Casilan, "for all to understand."

The procurator's lips thinned. A faint flush touched his ears.

"I am here," Cillian said to Casyn, "because I believe you have need of your adjutant. An important piece of information is being overlooked in these negotiations."

I got up and pulled out a chair. "Sit, Major." I offered my arm. Close to him, I could see the beads of sweat at his hairline, and the set of his jaw.

"I object to this man's presence," Decanius said.

He pushed his chair back to rise.

"As the Empress would object to your usurping of her authority," Cillian said.

Decanius's lip curled again. "Usurping her authority? I am the Procurator here, and the voice of the Empress in this province."

"Procurator, you are mistaken," Cillian said. Gods, I thought, do not be so direct. "This Western Empire is a Royal province, under Eudekia's direct oversight, and as such taxes and laws are the responsibility of the Governor, not a Procurator. The Governor who is not yet here."

The flush on the Procurator's face was spreading to his bald crown. "Until he is, they are mine to administer," Decanius said.

"They are not. They are the *Princip's*, until the Governor arrives. I negotiated the treaty, Procurator. I know what it says." The shaking in Cillian's hands was growing worse. "I must write to Eudekia, very soon. We became," he paused, "not what you implied earlier, but good friends in my time there, and I promised to let her know how we prospered as part of her Empire." His eyes were locked on Decanius's.

"You do not know Casil's laws," the Procurator said, dismissively. "How could you? I stand proxy to the Governor."

"I could also let her know what rumours you are spreading about the ties between the son of an Emperor, and the Empress you purport to serve."

Cillian said.

As unobtrusively as I could, I put one hand on Cillian's back. He leaned into it, just a little. He felt hot, feverish. I looked at Lena. She was watching him, her eyes frightened. "Water," I mouthed.

She brought the cup. He didn't look at her, his gaze fixed on Decanius. The Procurator's bald head gleamed red, now. He licked his lips. "All letters go by our ships."

Under my hand, I felt Cillian tense. The Procurator smiled.

"Not necessarily," I said. "There is another route, Procurator. The one I took to reach Casil."

He made no reply. No one spoke for a heartbeat, and then another.

"But of course," Cillian said quietly, "my memory sometimes falters." Tremors were running through his back now.

Decanius blinked. His mouth opened, closed, as if he searched for words. "What might bring on those lapses?"

"The skilled attention of my soldier-servant," Cillian said. "His ministrations so relax me, my mind wanders. My physician concurs, if you would prefer to ask him."

I glanced at Casyn. He was leaning forward, a hand over his mouth. Disguising a smile, I was sure.

Decanius turned to his scribe. "Give me paper." He scribbled a note. "Fetch me the soldier Druisius, from the infirmary. Give this to his guards."

No one spoke for the minutes it took the scribe to do as Decanius had ordered. I could feel Cillian's muscles clenching as he tried to control the tremors. "Water?" I whispered to him. He shook his head slightly. Under the table, his right hand found my knee.

Summoning a memory long suppressed. I had been sixteen, a man in Sorham, not a boy, but young. Cillian, in his role as *toscaire,* had come to see my father. One night we had music, and dancing, and as I played I had watched him dance, desire rising. He'd glanced over at me: our eyes had met. And when the dance was done, he'd come over to me, knelt in front of me to ask about the instrument. He'd reached out to touch my fingers on the neck of the *ladhar* with one hand. The other had rested on my knee, as if for balance.

I forced my mind to the present. Runnels of sweat wet Cillian's face. His hand on my knee tightened, almost to the point of pain.

No, I thought, fighting my body's unwanted reaction. No. Concentrate on why you are here. He has no idea what he is doing to you; it is to control his own desires, which have nothing to do with yours. Nor will they ever.

I put a hand over his. He let me take it, entwining his fingers with mine, squeezing hard. I didn't flinch. This, a friend could do.

Druisius's eyes went straight to Cillian when he

came in, his lips thin and tight. Then he saluted both the Procurator and Casyn, standing rigidly at attention. He did not look at me.

"Soldier," Decanius said. "A mistake has been made, due to records poorly kept in the heat of battle. That you requested and were given permission to transfer your service to the army of the Western Empire was—overlooked."

"And so we must remedy it," Casyn said. "You will swear allegiance to me, in front of these witnesses, Druisius. My scribe will record it, and the Procurator will sign, as will I, so there is no chance of future confusion. If you so wish, that is."

"I do, *Princip*," Druisius said. "Do I kneel?"

"No."

"I am Druisius of Casil," my lover said, following the words Casyn gave him to say. "On this day, released from my service to the Eastern Empire, I freely give my allegiance to Casyn, *Princip* of the Western Empire." Of his own accord, he added, "and to his heirs, born and unborn." I translated, wondering at the last part.

"I, Casyn, *Princip* of the Western Empire, accept your oath, Druisius." He turned to Lena. "Have you recorded that?"

"In our language, *Princip*."

"Lord Sorley?" I wrote the translation and passed it to Decanius's scribe to check. He nodded. Casyn signed, and then Decanius. The Procurator stood, immediately.

"A satisfactory conclusion," he said, not meaning it at all. "I am keeping the lands, of course."

CHAPTER 16

THE MOMENT THE DOOR shut behind him, Druise was at Cillian's side. "Give me that water," he ordered. Cillian had stopped trying to control the tremors. Sweat ran down his face. Gnaius appeared from the other room, holding out a vial. Had he been there the entire time? Druise mixed its contents with the water. "Drink," he ordered, holding it to Cillian's lips. "*Idióta*. Six hours ago you should have had this."

"I needed a clear mind." He swallowed the drug. Druise got up, moving aside for Lena. She put her arms around Cillian, one hand stroking his hair, whispering to him. He pulled her closer, but his hand was still in mine. Gnaius stood, watching him.

Slowly the tremors subsided, and his breathing became steadier. Druise had disappeared into the back room, returning with a damp cloth. He wiped Cillian's face. "*Idióta*," he said again, but this time he was smiling. "Thank you."

Cillian almost grinned. "Don't thank me," he said. "It was your question this morning that made me realize. Druise," he said to the rest of us, "asked me what sort of province we were. Casil has two types of provinces: ones administered by the officials, and Royal provinces which belong to the Empress. In the former case, the Procurator is often also the Governor. But never in Royal provinces, which is what we are."

"Did you know this?" Casyn asked, turning to me.

"I saw the words in the treaty," I said slowly. "I did not know what they meant."

"I knew this was a Royal province," Gnaius said. "The Empress would not have sent me, otherwise. But that you did not understand the implications, no. I am sorry, *Princip*. I could have saved you worry."

Cillian sat up a little straighter, releasing my hand so he could rest his on the curve of Lena's belly. She covered it with one of hers.

"You did know," Casyn said to him, "didn't you? That was why you hadn't told us the Procurator would arrive: he wasn't that important."

"I had told the Emperor," Cillian said, "but, yes. The man should never have taken the power he has; his work was to be counting and mapping. I could not make the connections between what Sorley or you told me, and what was happening, not while the poppy dimmed my mind."

"You couldn't see the game board," I said.

"Exactly."

I got up, touching his shoulder as I walked behind him to put my arms around Druise. "*Amané*," I murmured, "I was so worried." A surge of something I couldn't name ran through me, something deeper than relief. Could I ever atone for what I had thought?

"I was not," Druise said, stepping back from my embrace. "The gods decide."

"You, my friend," Cillian said, "are a better follower of Catilius than I am, I think. But perhaps I have repaid a tiny portion of the debt I owe to Sorley today."

"You would have," I said, "had there been one owed. *Meas*, Cillian. *Meas, mo charaidh gràhadh*."

"Kiss your *quincala*," Gnaius told him, "and then we go back to the infirmary. Six or seven more days, if you have not done too much damage today."

"Before you go," Casyn said, "what did Decanius say to you at the beginning? And what language was that?"

Cillian smiled. "He called me, effectively, a *scraptus*. A man who sells his body. He had not expected me to understand, as I had no Heræcrian when I met with his uncle in Casil. Gnaius has remedied that, for which I have Sorley to thank, I believe."

∰

A week later Druise came to find me, late in the evening. "He has done it," he told me. "Five days now since the last tiny dose, and the sweating and nausea and fever are all gone. Now," he shrugged, "it will be his strength of will, and our help, that will keep him free of it."

I wrapped my arms around him. "You must be exhausted, Druise," I said.

"Not too bad. I could sleep, these last few days, when Cillian did. Lena can see him tomorrow, I think."

"And they can marry, now he is free of the poppy. Are you going to bed now?"

"Yes." He yawned. "Sleep, nothing else. You go to Cillian. I would not wake Lena; the morning is soon enough." Lena, I thought, would not agree. And perhaps I would override Druise's decision, after I had seen Cillian.

He looked thinner even than the week before, and there were dark circles under his eyes, but he was himself. Calm and reflective, clearly in some pain, but wholly Cillian, in a way he had not been since Druisius had come to fetch me, almost five months previously.

"Sorley," he said. "Help me stand. I just need your arm, to steady me." I held it out. He brought himself to his feet, one hand on my forearm. "Come." I stepped into the embrace, tears threatening.

"*Mo duíne gràhadh*," I murmured. "I am so glad to

see you well."

"Thank Druisius," he said. "And Gnaius. Without them, I would not be." He released me, studying my face in the low light of the room. "We have much to talk about. I remember most of what you have told me over the months, and what I said to you—or I believe I do—but it feels distant. As if I responded with only part of my mind. Will you forgive me for that?"

"Do not," I said, "be a fool, Cillian. You cannot ask forgiveness for the effects of a drug your physician prescribed and would not allow you to forgo."

He laughed. *Laughed.* "Perhaps not. Gnaius tells me I will want poppy when the pain is bad for a very long time, perhaps years," he added in a graver voice. "That my desire for it will overrule my judgement and control."

"It certainly didn't, the afternoon you bested Decanius," I pointed out.

"I could not have gone on much longer, and not at all without you beside me. It is not in my nature to ask for help, but I believe I may need it, occasionally."

"I will be here," I said, reflexively. Well, I would be, for some time.

"Your constancy, my lord Sorley, is welcomed," he said, a faint smile playing on his lips. My formal title had the sound of an endearment. "Now, tell me your thoughts about Decanius."

"Cillian," I protested, "not now. I thought I would

come to see you, then fetch Lena."

"Let her sleep. She needs her rest. Decanius troubles me. I have made an enemy there, and so, I think, have you, for yourself and for Linrathe. I worry for our lands, because I believe this Procurator wants nothing less than complete Casilani control, and that was not what the Empress and I discussed, nor what the treaties were meant to give."

"Won't it depend on who the Governor is, now you've clarified this is a Royal province?" I settled into a chair. If Cillian wanted to talk about politics—before seeing Lena?—then I would concede.

"It may. What concerns me is that the things Eudekia and I spoke of were not recorded, made official. She was intrigued by what I could tell her of how women and men lived here; the separate lives and responsibilities. It was not her intent in ending the Partition agreement to destroy that, only to give more choice to both. Much what my father wanted."

"I wouldn't know."

"He told me of his ideas, in the nights we spent talking at the Eastern Fort. He wanted no more boys castrated for not being able to fight, as his brother had been. He saw Colm in me, he said. I could have suffered the same fate, had he known of my birth while I was still a child, and claimed me."

"Fighting is not that hard, Cillian."

"No? I have only once known the impulse to violence, Sorley, and it was directed towards a man already dead."

"Because you are thinking theoretically," I said. "When a man with a sword or axe is swinging it at you, your impulses change. Believe me."

"Perhaps they do," he said. "I did kill a bear once, when it would not listen to calm words and a reasoned approach." I heard the dry, self-mocking tone, and grinned. "But I felt remorse, even though it would have killed us for no reason except that we were between it and the water it wanted. And Lena—" He shook his head. "Killing did not grow easier for her, Sorley."

"Except Fritjof," I said.

"Has she told you that?"

"No. She has never mentioned it, and I assumed—after everything he or his men did—"

"I wonder," he said softly. "But to return to Decanius. Assuming the Governor—who should arrive very soon—is of like mind, exactly what are they demanding?"

We spoke of the Procurator and his dictatorial approach to what he saw necessary to make the Western Empire a 'modern province of Casil' as he so constantly put it. I told him of the surveys and censuses and maps, and plans for vast estates, and men brought from Casil to oversee them.

"The army, he says, must be completely re-organized: the ranks brought into line with Casil's, and women's cohorts limited to archery, as they are there," I told Cillian. "The *Princip* has agreed to the first, reluctantly, but is rejecting the second." I watched him assimilate the information. "What do you think they will ask of Linrathe?" I asked.

He shook his head. "I do not know. Some subtle way of gaining influence? Or simple military force? The former is my guess, but until we know more of the Governor, it remains a supposition. But there will be much work for me to do here." The lamp flickered and guttered; the oil was running low. "The *Ti'ach* will have to wait, I am afraid."

"Then it waits," I said. I wouldn't mind. Not at all. But what would Lena think? She had been adamant she wanted to bring up their child in Linrathe.

"What will you do in this land?" he asked.

"Teach languages, probably," I said. "And I am still Linrathe's *toscaire*. It's very late. Shouldn't you sleep?"

"I doubt I will," he said. He grimaced, moving his leg.

"You are in pain. What can I do?"

"Nothing more than what you are doing. Talking distracts me."

"Is there willow-bark here? If I make tea, will you drink it?"

He smiled. "If you will play *xache* with me while it steeps, yes." His easy capitulation surprised me. He told me where the supplies were, and I busied myself making tea while he, refusing my assistance, rose to limp to a sideboard to retrieve the game. "I taught Druisius; did he tell you?" he asked as he set up the pieces.

"No. We have not had much time to talk," I said, pouring hot water on the shredded bark. I set the pot beside the brazier. "Is he any good?"

"Not yet. He is prone to taking risks. But teaching him was another distraction."

We played the game. After some time I brought Cillian the tea, but regardless of his pain I was losing badly at that point, and he had me defeated in only a few more moves. His game had been precise and deliberate, and I knew I'd never really had a chance. As he made the final victorious move, I laughed. "I have never been so happy to lose," I said.

"Callan and I played a few times," he said thoughtfully. "He was better than I, or perhaps more truthfully his strategies were not ones I knew. I wish—" He stopped. *Do not wish for a different fate*, Catilius would say. But I do. I wish he had not died, for the sake of his land, and his brother, and because we were beginning to be friends."

"At least you had some time with him," I said, "time to talk, to understand and accept each other."

"Not in all ways. I accepted, and forgave, that his oath to his country had superseded his love for my mother. He had been very young, and the penalty was death. We had not discussed in any detail why I, somewhat older, had betrayed mine. I would like to have had that talk."

"Would you? I can think of nothing worse than

having a similar discussion with my father."

"Asking Callan to acknowledge me was not the betrayal," Cillian said, looking away from the fire, into the dark. *"No man, nor prince, nor foreign power has sway over me, and my loyalty is to the people of Linrathe, and the land beneath my feet."*

"Given the treaty you convinced Eudekia to sign regarding Linrathe," I said, "I'm sure you have atoned for anything you might see as betrayal. In my father's eyes, if he knows, I have betrayed him simply by being who I am. Nothing I can ever make up for, unless I deny my nature, and marry and father children."

"Catilius," Cillian said, "would say then that you loved yourself too little, or you would love what your nature asks of you."

"Cillian," I said, yawning, "It is far too late for philosophy."

"You are taking me to task?" he answered, lightly. "As you should. I am keeping you from your bed, and you have work to do in the morning."

Reluctantly I stood, finishing the last drops of wine in my cup. "You should sleep too." I bent to drop a kiss on his head. He grasped my arm, resting his temple against my cheek for a moment.

"Perhaps I too need to consider Catilius's words," he murmured.

"Cannot we both just be content with what we have, at least for a little while?" I said, straightening. "You are alive, and recovering, and you have Lena, and the baby very soon."

His hand was still on my arm. "And you, *mo duíne gràhadh?*"

My beloved man. A sudden restriction my throat made my voice hoarse. "I have enough," I managed to say, "being here. With you. And I might be able to be a *scáeli* after all."

He looked up at me, his eyes unreadable in the flickering light. "You are one, in my mind. I know the dark gods well now; they wanted me, and without your music they would have me still. I fear for you, for the price they will demand in return."

"Don't," I said. Something clawed at my heart, stripping away defences and arguments. "Don't fear, Cillian. You are worth any price to me." The inexorable, inevitable truth. How could I have denied it?

"You believe that now," he said. "But a reckoning will come, for all of us, for the choices we have made. You may think differently then. Go and sleep. I will see you in the morning."

In the corridor outside I turned right, away from the direction of my room. I let myself into the sitting room before knocking gently on the bedroom door. When I heard Lena's sleepy question, I opened it and went in. "Sorley?"

"I have just left Cillian," I told her. "He is awake, and free, and himself, Lena."

She slid out of bed, pushing her feet into soft

slippers, hurrying from the room. I stood quietly for a few moments, watching her, before I closed the door.

THE CHARACTERS OF *ORAIÁPHON*

Characters who are a direct part of the story are in
bold. Characters who are mentioned by name but not
directly a part of the story are in plain type.

Asgaill – a *Comiádh* of Linrathe
Birel – Casyn's soldier-servant
Bren – a General of the Empire
Callan – the Emperor of the West, deceased; Cillian's
father
Casyn – a General of the Empire, Callan's brother, now
Princip
Cillian –Callan's son, Lena's partner; Major of the
Empire; adjutant to the *Princip*
Colm – Callan's twin and advisor, deceased
Dagney – a woman of Sorham, the Lady of the *Ti'ach na
Perras*, *scáeli* and teacher
Decanius – Procurator, Quintus's nephew
Dern – an officer of the Empire, Captain of *Skua* and
Commander of the Northern Fleet
Donnalch – a *Teannasach* of Linrathe, deceased
Druisius – a soldier of Casil; Sorley's partner
Eudekia – the Empress of Casil and the East
Fritjof – *Härskaran* of the Marai of Varsland, deceased
Galen – Lena's father, a border scout
Garth – a Watch-Commander of the Empire, Maya's
brother
Gille – a woman of Tirvan, briefly Casyn's lover
Gnaius – a physician of Casil and Wall's End Fort
Gundar – Harr of Gundarstorp, Sorley's father
Gwen – a midwife and healer of Tirvan, Lena's mother,
deceased
Hafwen (Wenna) – a girl of Linrathe, Cillian's mother,
deceased

Irmgard – a princess of the Marai, now in Casil
Jereme – a Cadet-Master of the Empire
Jesa – a woman of Berge
Jordis – a girl of Linrathe, student at the *Ti'ach na Perras,* captured by the Marai
Junia – a woman of Casil, Captain of the horse archers
Kebhan – a boy of Linrathe, son to Lorcann, deceased
Kira – a woman of Tirvan, Lena's sister
Lena – a Lieutenant of the Empire, Cillian's partner
Liam – Ruar's great-uncle, and his regent (Raséair)
Lorcann – the *Teannasach* of Linrathe, deceased
Maya – a woman of Casilla, once Lena's partner
Michan – a Major of the Empire, adjutant to the *Princip*
Niav – a girl of Linrathe, Isa's niece, captured by the Marai
Perras – a man of Linrathe, the *Comiádh* of the *Ti'ach na Perras*
Phaulius – a Casilani soldier, aide to Decanius
Quintus – a man of Casil, advisor to Eudekia, uncle to Decanius
Randall – a man of Linrathe, language tutor and translator
Roghan – Sorley's brother
Ruar – a boy of Linrathe, Donnalch's son, next *Teannasach*
Rufin – a Casilani ship's captain
Sorley – musician; envoy for Linrathe; Druisius's partner
Tali – a woman of Tirvan, Pel and Maya and Garth's mother, deceased
Talyn – a Captain of the Empire, Casyn's daughter
Turlo – a General of the Empire

THE VOCABULARY OF *ORAIÁPHON*

The languages spoken in the *Empire's Legacy* series are my inventions, but they are based on existing or historic languages. Pronunciations and grammar may not follow the conventions of those languages. Roughly, Casilan is based on Latin; Linrathan primarily from Gaelic, both Scottish and Irish, and Marái'sta from Scandinavian languages.

Each word is followed by its pronunciation and then its meaning.

allech'i – *alek-i* – please
amané – *ah-man-eh* – lover (male)
an dithës braithréan – *ann dith-ess bray-trey-an* – the two brothers
anash – *ah-nash* – herb used against fever and conception
athàir – *athe-arr* – father
capora – *ka-porr-ah* – corporal
channàdarra – *chan-na-darr-ah* – literally, unnatural; a gay man
cithar – *kith-ar* – stringed instrument, zither
Comiádh – *ko-mi-ath* – professor
consor – *kon-sorr* – partner
danta – *dan-tha* – saga
dùthcas– *duuth-chas* – belonging, heredity
Eirën/Eirënnen – *ayr-en/ayr-en-en* –landholder(s), lord(s) (male)
fuisce – *vwi-schah* – whiskey
Harr/Härren – harr/hurren – landholder(s), lord(s) (male)
Härra – *hurra* – landholder, lady (s/pl) (female)
idióta – *id-ee-oh-ta* – idiot

käresta/kärestan – *ka-resta/kares-tan* – beloved
Konë – *konn-uh* – landholder, lady (s/pl) (female)
ladhar – *lath-arr* – lute
li'ítho – *lee-ito* – marriage bracelet
Marái'sta – *mar-uh-ee-stah* – of the Marai (referring to language)
mathàir – *mathe-arr* – mother
meas – *may-as* – thank you
mensore(s) – *men-sore-eh(s)* – surveyor(s)
mo bhráithar – *mo vra-ith-arr* – my brother
mo charaidh – *mo kar-aith* – my friend
mo charaidh gràhadh – *mo kar-aith gra-hath* – my beloved   friend
mo duíne gràhadh – *mo du-inne gra-hath* – my beloved man
mo gràhadh – *mo gra-hath* – my beloved
quincala/quincalum– *kin-call-ah/kin-call-um* – freely-chosen partner
raséair – *rah-shair* – regent
scáeli – *schaa-lee* – bard
scraptus – *scrap-tus* – male prostitute
Teannasach – *tee-na-shah* – chieftain, leader
Teannas'og – *tee-na-shog* **–** little leader
thá – *thah* – yes (literally, 'is')
thà mi gràh agäthe – *ta me grah ag-ut-eh* – I love you
ti'ach(a) – tee-ach(ah) – college(s)
Ti'ach na Asgaill, Ti'ach na Perras – college of Asgaill, college of   Perras, used to indicate which *Ti'ach*
torp – *torp* – land held by an *Eirën* or *Harr*
torpari – *tor-par-ee* – farmworkers, peasants
toscaire/toscairen – *tos-care/tos-car-en* – envoy/envoys
xache – *za-chee* – game similar to chess
zinkolo – *zink-olo* – male prostitute

ACKNOWLEDGMENTS

As always, thanks are due to many people: my fellow writers at The Writing Room; members of Guelph Genre Group; and Luke Hill and the Vocamus Writers' Community, all for fostering an environment that encourages and supports writers. My fellow members of Arboretum Press Collective must always be thanked, for their enthusiasm, tolerance, and critical thoughts.

Special thanks to my cover designer, Anthony O'Brien, who always creates a cover that looks exactly like what I had in mind.

To Terrence Thomas, who acted as developmental editor, and Bjørn Larssen, beta/sensitivity reader, my deepest appreciation for pointing out flaws and suggesting solutions. Bjørn especially insisted I examine the relationship between Sorley and Druisius more closely, and also told me to stop making Sorley so nice. Any remaining errors, in content or structure, are my own. Terry, I hope Aristotle would approve now.

Finally, my husband Brian Rennie, my critique partner, has listened to me talk about this story for nearly eighteen months, with remarkable patience and insight. Without him, *Oraiáphon* would not be. Period.

EMPIRE'S DAUGHTER

"...easily one of the most intriguing books I've read
all year..."

Writerlea Book Reviews

"Empire's Daughter is a story that enriches the
imagination. A compelling tale of survival and strength
in unity."

Avril Borthiry, author of *Triskelion*

"...expertly builds an entire world and an entire
society..."

Bjørn Larssen, author of *Storytellers*

"Within the first few pages, I realized I'd stumbled
upon a truly special story; for Thorpe has created an
alternative world that bends gender and sexual norms
in brilliant form."

Two Doctors Media Collaborative

EMPIRE'S HOSTAGE

"A bold vision of historical fantasy written
beautifully from start to finish; *Empire's Hostage* takes
us on an epic journey that is at once intriguing,
convincing, and deeply affecting."

Jonathan Ballagh, author of *The Quantum Door*

"Empire's Hostage is as immersive as Marian L Thorpe's first book *Empire's Daughter*. Filled with beautiful imagery and well-developed, realistic characters, *Empire's Hostage* surpassed my expectations. "

D.M. Wiltshire, author of the *Prophecy Six* series

"With its multidimensional protagonist and its vivid rendering of her world, *Empire's Hostage* elevates the genre."

Maria Luisa Lang, author of *The Pharaoh's Cat*

EMPIRE'S EXILE

"nothing short of brilliance…"

Cover to Cover Book Reviews

"*Empire's Exile* might be Marian L. Thorpe's finest work so far…. [it] is a lot of things – a romance, a psychological study, a painting or rather a movie, a world so real that the book feels like historical fiction."

Bjørn Larssen, author of *Storytellers*

Visit my website:
marianlthorpe.com
find me on Facebook
https://www.facebook.com/marianthorpe/
Twitter
@marianlthorpe

www.ingramcontent.com/pod-product-compliance
Lightning Source LLC
Chambersburg PA
CBHW021133190726
48288CB00008B/2627